for
Bo
Bob Parr.
10/12/2019

BLOOD
on the
IRON HARD GROUND

A story of Love in a time of War

BOB PARR

SO3
MEDIA

SO3 Media
Level One
13 Camp Street
Queenstown 9300
New Zealand

www.so3media.com

First published 2018

Copyright © Robert Parr 2018

Robert Parr asserts the moral right
to be identified as the author of this work

This novel is a work of fiction.
The names and characters portrayed in it are
the work of the author's imagination. Any resemblance to
actual persons, living or dead, is entirely coincidental.
Submitted for Disclosure review and approved for publication

A catalogue record for this book is available
from the British Library

ISBN: 978 1 68 454744 9

All rights reserved. No part of this publication may be
reproduced, stored in a retrieval system, or transmitted in any form
by any means, electronic, mechanical, photocopying, recording or
otherwise, without the prior permission of the publishers

For Muki

PROLOGUE

The child made her way across the city park, stooping here and there to rummage through some discarded bag of trash or pile of rotting junk in the hope of finding something useful that she could take home. A gentle wind cut through her threadbare clothes, and though the morning air was far from cold she shivered and pulled her thin jacket close around her shoulders. We watched through our binoculars, adjusting focus so we could see her better, sharp and clear.

The underlying soil was hard and dry, baked solid by the summer sun. Thousands of footprints were petrified in the ground, footprints that described patterns around ugly, filth-strewn craters. The avenues of this park were once lined with trees, splendid in the summer and golden in the fall. But the trees had long-since been de-limbed or felled; fuel for the stove, heat for the home during winter. Just a few ugly stumps remained, pock-marked with bullet holes, scarred by shrapnel.

The attacks had started during the night, NATO jets targeting Serb positions all around the city perimeter and United Nations artillery pounding their positions closer in. Now there was a pause, but most of Sarajevo's tired population had gone to ground because the Serbs would surely respond. They always did.

It seemed incongruous to me that such a young child should be wandering alone and vulnerable at such a time. Somebody should have swept her up, taken care of her, made sure she was safe.

We adjusted focus again and could see that the young girl had spotted something with her beautiful, mysterious eyes. She paused, reached down, and then carefully lifted a piece of wood as if it were a precious object of art. She broke away a few clods of soil and then placed her prize in a small canvas bag slung across her slim shoulders, using all the tenderness that a caring mother might show to her newborn child.

A fleeting expression of triumph passed across her pale, thin face, and the faintest hint of a smile creased the side of her pretty mouth. Then her head exploded, torn from her shoulders by a sniper's bullet fired from a mile away across the front line.

We saw this from our vantage point, safe in our heavily guarded position. We saw the girl's body collapse, spurting bright arterial blood into the air. We saw the ebb tide of life flow from her twitching corpse, darkening and congealing on the iron-hard ground.

And for all our sophistication and firepower, and pompous international mandates drafted and ratified by the most powerful men on Earth, there was nothing that we could do. Nothing we could do at all, apart from weep.

CHAPTER 1

The inside of the French armoured personnel carrier was as cold as a tomb and our breath was condensing heavily on the air. In the eerie grey moonlight filtering through the gunports, I could see a thin layer of frost on every exposed metal surface. I shifted my backside in a vain attempt to improve my comfort, but everything was numb apart from my aching back.

The Frenchmen, kneeling or half-standing on their seats with their rifles poking out, had the strange appearance of a firing squad taking aim on an execution detail as their gimlet eyes surveyed the scene outside through misted weapon sights. We had been here for hours by now, and they had barely flinched. Perhaps their excessive zeal was due to the presence of two Englishmen, thrown in with them at the last moment as a gesture of bilateral cooperation, an attempt at military *détente*.

"Do they think we're unprofessional?" I asked Bagley.

Languid, disinterested Bagley; Private First Class.

"Do you think I care?" he replied.

Silence again.

"I feel the need to beat retreat," I said.

"We're sticking with the French until this is over," said Bagley. "That's what the major told us."

'The major isn't here," I replied, pointedly. 'The major isn't freezing his arse off, stuck on a mountainside with a bunch of Frenchmen who can't even provide their guests with a warm brew on a cold night."

The French soldier alongside me aimed a sharp kick at my ribs.

"Ros bif!"

"You understand English?" I asked.

"Ros bif!" he said again, but this time I avoided his boot.

Presently the man stepped down from his position, and with a loud sigh parked his backside on a seat. Bagley offered him a smoke that he accepted with a nonchalant shrug. Then one by one the Frenchmen abandoned their posts, delighted that all their macho posturing was spent.

One of them produced a flask of *Slivovica*, a locally brewed plum brandy that was strong enough to propel rockets. This he passed freely from hand to hand, laughing at us when we spluttered and coughed, topping it up from some kind of bladder stashed in his backpack whenever it ran dry. We laughed along with him, but quietly so the officer in the front of the vehicle couldn't hear.

"Why are we stuck on this godforsaken hill?" asked Bagley.

The Frenchman who had kicked me in the ribs grunted. "Because this is what we have been told to do." His accent was Gallic, but his English was good. "A French soldier does what he is told to do, no questions."

"We've been told that the Muslims are breaching the Demilitarised Zone," I said. "That they may be provoking the Serbs."

"The Serbs need to be provoked," replied the Frenchman. "Because they are evil men."

This must be the truth, because it's what the BBC had been telling us.

"What do you think the Muslims are doing?" I asked.

"Repaying a debt of blood," said the Frenchman, melodramatically.

"Giving the Serbs a good spanking," said Bagley, pragmatically.

The French soldier cracked a small chemical stick, and in a moment the inside of the APC was bathed in muted green light. "The Bosnians went over the mountain to split a few skulls," he said. "To make a point."

"So, what are we meant to be doing about it?" asked Bagley.

"Reporting on their movements," replied the Frenchman.

"Not stopping them?"

"Of course not. We're not here to fight a war."

There was a general murmur of agreement. Evidently a number of these men could understand English.

"And if they shoot at us?" I asked.

"Then we shoot back," replied the Frenchman.

There was a louder murmur of assent.

We were silent for a while, rubbing our cold hands together and stamping our frozen toes upon the floor. The vapour of our breath and the smoke from our cigarettes filled the vehicle with a dense fug. Then the wind began to pick-up, and frost-laden air blasted in through the gun-ports.

"I need to pee," said Bagley.

"You must use the *pissoir*," said the French soldier, motioning towards a tin can with a wide funnel attached to its lid. But Bagley pushed open the back door and stepped into the night because he had no intention of parading his manhood in full view of the French Army.

"I'll join you," I said, and before anyone could intervene followed Bagley outside.

The night was surprisingly bright, and I could see the blurred outline of a silver moon through a blanket of low-lying cloud that was pregnant with snow. The bleak shoulder of Mount Igman curved away to the south, and the surrounding countryside was bathed in a pale, diffused light. Bagley and I stepped off the road and stood close together, peeing into the snow, watching our urine smoke and splutter in the rising wind.

"Funny bunch, huh?" I said.

"They know more about this place that we do".

"That's not hard."

We shook ourselves dry, holstered our pride and headed towards the carrier.

"Allez! Allez!"

The officer was leaning out of the vehicle's front door, gesturing for us to get back inside. We didn't need encouraging. It was seriously cold out there.

Another hour drifted by, largely in silence apart from the occasional passage of gastric wind or the flicking of a cigarette lighter. The temperature dropped further. We sat and shivered, huddling together for mutual warmth, lost in our thoughts or drifting through dreams.

Around three in the morning, a Frenchman stood on his seat and peered out. He grabbed his rifle.

"Attention! Attention!"

We scrambled to our feet. This time Bagley and I managed to claim a gun-port between us, and our eyes opened wide to accommodate the darkness. The fairytale moon had disappeared and the night seemed harsh and sinister.

Then we saw them.

Descending through the gloom along the winding, snow-covered road came a long column of Bosnian soldiers. Soldiers fresh from battle; soldiers carrying heavy machine guns and tripods and mortar tubes and rocket launchers, soldiers with the hunched look of men beyond exhaustion; soldiers who had seen too much and done too much.

Closer they came, and now I could see their faces, smeared with dirt and pinched with cold. Faces that were grimly set; faces from which bright eyes burned with hatred and bitter determination; faces that were old before their time. Some of the men carried the bounty of war - bottles of wine, radios, clothing; the personal effects of the dead.

There was a gasp from the French soldiers at something they had been told over their personal radio sets. They exchanged horrified looks, clutched at their weapons and resumed their aim.

I grabbed the English-speaking Frenchman by his shoulder.

"What is it?"

"The officer says they surprised the Serbs in their beds. Butchered them and burned them, cut the throats of women... *Ces hommes sont des démons!*"

My mouth went dry as I peered out into the night. I squirmed as the Bosnian soldiers filed past, silent and deadly; hundreds of them, maybe a thousand or more. Some were wearing black scarves knotted around their heads. Dangerous, cunning, ruthless and alive; staring up at us with their fathomless dark eyes deep-set in their sallow, empty faces.

And our lone white vehicle, with its United Nations logo stencilled proudly on its side and the muzzles of our rifles poking ridiculously through its gun-ports, seemed small, powerless and vulnerable; a tin-can joke perched on the side of this ghostly hill, a chunk of useless metal stuffed full of frightened men.

Then they were gone, so we sat down once more and smoked cigarettes and finished off the *Slivovica* and rubbed our frozen hands in contemplative silence until dawn arrived and the officer told us we'd been ordered to drive back down to the city.

CHAPTER 2

Around this time the Serbs began applying greater pressure on the besieged Muslims by letting off the occasional mortar round into Sarajevo and increasing their concentration of sniper fire across the front line. It was all highly unnerving, and morale wasn't much improved by the British general in charge of the UN Forces who declared that it would be every man for himself if things became too hot, and that the evacuation plan for his headquarters would require a mass exodus of staff on foot across Mount Igman, headed for some indeterminate rendezvous in Croatia more than one hundred kilometres distant.

Bagley and I had been assigned to the general's staff in Tito's old Residency with the UN Observers. The Observers were something akin to dispatch riders, men who carried the general's authority in passing messages, facilitating liaison and picking up any number of other duties. I didn't know why we'd been assigned to this task, it was just something we'd been told to do.

The arrangement suited us, for otherwise we would have been immersed in the tedium of convoy protection, stuck for days or even weeks at Serb or Muslim or Croat checkpoints, bored beyond reckoning, frustrated beyond belief. Instead, acting on the authority of the British general, we could often negotiate our way between the warring factions and even past the French; though with the French, tasked as they were by the United Nations in policing the city, things could be more difficult.

So the weeks passed, and we gradually came to know better the city with its shattered buildings and dislocated infrastructure, its underground cafes and treeless parks; its intermittently operating tram system and cratered roads. We learned how to negotiate the suburbs with a careful eye to the possibility of being targeted by snipers, and to navigate in part by recognising key landmarks and in part by sheer intuition.

So it was that we came to realise the men and women of the United Nations were in many respects just as much hostages in this grey place as the city's own sad inhabitants.

One day, Bagley and I were sent to the airport. We drove slowly from checkpoint to checkpoint. Counter-sniper screens along the route comprised long lines of bullet-riddled cars and shattered buses piled one on top another, row after row of them, strengthened in places by rusted sheets of mild steel welded together or by metal filing cabinets filled with hardened cement. People traversing this area on foot were pressed up against these screens, carrying their bundled possessions or bags of firewood that they'd foraged from the surrounding area, running awkwardly wherever there were gaps, clearly relieved when they made it safely to the other side.

The airport terminal, such as it was, was crowded and noisy. The UN's Norwegian contingent had primacy here, tall men with pale blue eyes and fair hair. They were invariably good mannered, but quite determined that everybody should abide by their rules. They stamped both incoming and outgoing passports with the legend 'Maybe Airlines', which was an accurate reflection of the varying certainties that applied to the likelihood, or otherwise, of your flight arriving in sequence, on time… or even at all.

"What do you think she'll look like?" asked Bagley.

"Blonde hair, blue eyed and beautiful," I replied.

But I was wrong about the officer. She was raven-haired, grey-eyed and rather plain. She was wearing shapeless combat fatigues, an impossibly large flak jacket and a blue United Nations beret. Her hair was rolled tightly into a bun on the back of her head, and her accent was rather jolly-hockey-sticks, frightfully English.

"You're with the Observers?" she asked as I reach her through the crowd.

"Yes, ma'am." I threw up a salute.

"I'm Lieutenant Harris."

"We were sent to meet you."

She insisted on carrying her own backpack, even though it looked impossibly heavy for her slight frame.

"Been in Bosnia long?" she asked.

"Just a few weeks, ma'am."

She offloaded her pack into the Land Rover and said, "Super. I'll drive."

"I don't think…" began Bagley, but she cut him short.

"Don't worry, Private. I know the way."

"Bagley. My name's Bagley." He sounded hurt, but climbed into the back anyway.

We took off, and it quickly became evident that Lieutenant Harris really did know the way. She knew it better than us, and she drove very well. In no time at all we were closing with the city centre, traveling so fast that moment by moment I feared we might break a half-shaft or strip a tyre as the Land Rover bumped and squealed its way along the potholed roads.

The lieutenant had one of those personalities that is bubbly and intense, and a vocabulary that was strewn with *super-duper* and *righty-ho* and *absolutely, buster*. I was amazed that she'd survived her first tour in Bosnia because she exuded a naïve charm that would more comfortably have been at home amongst the Hooray Henrys of Sloane Street in London. I wondered how long she would last in the general's headquarters.

"This place is *soooo* much quieter than when I was here before," she said. "Last time it was on *fire*…"

"It can still be quite racy, ma'am," I said.

"Oh, quit with the ma'am stuff," she said, swerving to avoid a particularly large crater. "You can call me Lieutenant. And don't salute me, snipers *love* to take shots at people who are being saluted."

"Yes ma'am… Lieutenant."

Later that afternoon I was told to escort the lieutenant on a city orientation. Bagley was highly displeased when I told him that he was not required because the lieutenant would be driving. It didn't take long for me to figure that the lieutenant would do just fine in the general's headquarters. First of all, she could speak fluent Serbo-Croat, which was probably the main reason for her being here at all. But more than that, she had a solid understanding of the politics and history of the place.

She drove us quickly and accurately to an urban ridgeline that commanded a first-class overlook of the city. It was a place I'd not been to before, an area of wasteland that looked across towards the Serb-controlled suburb of Grbavica. She parked the Land Rover at the top of the tarmac road and we walked higher onto the ridge along a frozen, mudded track until we had a clear view of the city below. She walked faster than I'd expected, and I struggled to keep up. Off to our left were two burned-out office blocks, twenty floors high and with every window shattered.

"Both of those were burning last time I was up here," she said. "They were full of Bosnian Government staff. It was quite a sight."

"It must have been hell."

"It was. The Serbs came right into the city with their tanks, all the way onto the main road down there. They took over the Presidency too, at one point."

She stopped walking and stood with her hands on her hips, looking towards the road, pensive. I hadn't noticed until then how slim her waist was.

"The trams used to run along there," she continued. "But then the Serbs started shooting them up, and they had to stop."

"Why don't these people simply stop all this completely?" I asked. "Even a civil war has to end somewhere, doesn't it? Surely they have to learn how to get along with each other?"

She took a sideways look at me and laughed. I could see I was wrong to think she had plain looks. She was attractive after all, in that English-rose kind of way; all fresh complexion and smiling eyes.

"You'll learn, Corporal," she said.

"Learn what?"

"The truth about this place."

She was walking again, higher yet along the ridgeline. I fell-in alongside her, glancing over my shoulder, a little anxious about the security of our abandoned vehicle. She stopped at the top of the ridge and jumped onto a lump of concrete. A chill wind plucked at her combats and for the first time I could see the full shape of her figure, which was finely proportioned - athletic perhaps, and wickedly attractive. It occurred to me that I'd been in the company of men for too long. I began to enjoy Sarajevo for the first time since I'd arrived here.

The lieutenant's head was now higher than mine, and I felt strangely inferior. She had no eyes for me, though. She was looking into the far distance towards the looming bulk of Mount Igman, lost in thought, shading her eyes against the watery afternoon sunlight with a finely manicured hand.

"How long were you here last time?" I asked.

"Too long."

"It was rough, huh?"

"At times. It was all very sad. So much death, so much destruction."

She jumped down from her vantage point, and we walked slowly back towards the Land Rover.

"Do you know how many people have died in this city?" she asked.

"I've no idea. Thousands, I should think."

"Perhaps tens of thousands. And many times that number wounded." Her voice was small, and suddenly she didn't seem such a lightweight to me. I'd been wrong to judge. She must have seen a lot of terrible things.

In the distance I could hear the early onset of gunfire.

"They're at it already," I observed.

"No change there, then."

The gunfire intensified a little, and now we were halfway along the ridge back towards our vehicle. Then two high velocity bullets cracked past, and I was on the ground seeking cover, *down, crawl, observe...*

But the lieutenant simply stood there, staring out towards the Serb lines as if challenging the snipers to try again, which they did. Now we were fair game, silhouetted on this goddam ridgeline, easy targets, illuminated by the afternoon sun.

"Ma'am, get down!"

She looked at me imperiously, mocking.

"They're a mile and a half away," she said. "More likely to miss than hit. You look ridiculous down there."

Another round cracked by, closer this time. But she didn't move, just continued to stand there like Queen Boadicea or something, staring across the divide.

After a minute or so with no further fire, I scrambled shakily to my feet. We walked to our vehicle, got in and drove away.

The lieutenant patted my thigh reassuringly and I thought at that moment that I might be in love.

CHAPTER 3

A few days later, I was assigned to Lieutenant Harris again. This time we had Bagley with us. The lieutenant permitted him to drive, partly because it was his job, but mostly because she was sensitive enough to see he would feel emasculated and useless otherwise.

The rear of the Land Rover was cramped and uncomfortable, but I really didn't mind sitting behind the passenger's seat because the lieutenant's hair smelled like lavender and after a long night fantasising about her, I was completely infatuated.

"We're headed for the Presidency," she said, and her voice sounded like a fresh mountain stream bubbling through an alpine meadow in spring.

It took less than ten minutes to drive to the Bosnian Presidency. We parked-up in a nearby side street to wait for the general.

"Bagley, would you be a dear and buy me some cigarettes?" she asked.

Bagley shot me a look, and I nodded. The lieutenant flicked him a handful of notes and he slinked off along the street.

"You smoke?" I asked.

"You don't approve?"

"I don't mind," I replied. "I smoke too, sometimes, when I'm nervous. I just didn't think you would."

"Why not?"

"Because you're too…" I hesitated because I was aware that she was a lieutenant and I was corporal, and that I needed to be respectful.

"Too what?" she asked.

"You're too good-looking."

She turned and looked me straight in the eye, which was unnerving but delicious.

"Are you flirting with me?"

"Am I permitted?"

"Certainly not. I'm an officer."

"Does that make a difference?"

"It makes all the difference."

"Didn't you send Bagley away on purpose?"

"I sent him away to buy cigarettes."

"Oh."

Then the convoy arrived, and our fleeting moment of intimacy was done. The lieutenant jumped out of the Land Rover and trotted across the street to join with the general and his bodyguard. They disappeared into the Presidency, striding past the heavily armed guards with a cursory nod as they saluted. The heavy black doors slammed shut behind them. Bagley returned a few moments later with the cigarettes and seemed terribly annoyed that she hadn't waited.

I knew the conference at the Presidency was going to last for an hour, so I suggested to Bagley that we should indulge in a hot beverage. We sat in a smoke-filled coffee house nearby. It was hung with paintings ornately framed with wood and glass gathered from shop windows that had been shattered by artillery fire. Many of the paintings appeared to be illuminated Madonnas, which seemed strange to me because the overwhelming majority of people on this side of the confrontation line were Muslim. Other pictures depicted the old marketplace of Baščaršija with its wooden stalls and open coffee stands.

"Do you want a beer?" asked Bagley.

"We're on duty."

"Who's to know?"

"I'll know," I said.

"That doesn't count."

"Of course it does. I'm a corporal and you're a private."

"And you're a prick," he said with conviction, lighting up a cigarette and blowing smoke towards my face.

I liked Bagley. He came from a different unit to me, an infantryman, but he was OK for all that. There was something about his irreverent personality I admired. But I could see why he was still a private even though he must have been in his early thirties.

"Are you always insubordinate?" I asked.

"Only with pricks."

I couldn't help but laugh. "Maybe we can have the one beer," I said.

"Good man!"

He made for the bar, shouldering his way through a crowd of sour-smelling locals without apology. It's strange, I thought, that no matter how tough the times, there always seemed to be plenty of beer and cigarettes in this place.

Exactly an hour since we left, we were back on station outside the Presidency. A few minutes later its door opened, the sentries threw up a couple of disinterested salutes and the bodyguard emerged, closely followed by the general and Lieutenant Harris. The three of them paused on the sidewalk talking animatedly, though the bodyguard remained observant and alert, hand on his holstered pistol. Moments later the general's convoy pulled-up and they all climbed onboard and then drove away.

I felt disappointed and more than a little deflated. For the first time since arriving here, I resented not being part of the general's inner circle.

Back at the Residency there seemed to be a crisis brewing. The major was in something of a dizzy spin. He was in and out of the general's office a dozen times or more, speaking over the satphone, passing messages up and down his chain of command. Outside, the sound of sniper fire was picking-up even though it was barely lunchtime.

Bagley and I took up our usual position in the main building outside the kitchen, ever hopeful of grabbing a tea or a coffee should the head waiter or the cook have one on the brew. They made a strange pair, the waiter and the cook. They were locals, hired-in by the UN civil secretariat that had ultimate responsibility for the headquarters. Bagley and I theorised that they must have been Muslim spies, placed there by Bosnian Intelligence to report on everything we did and, if called upon to do so, to assassinate the general.

This was a great game to play, and provided us endless hours of fun as we tried to guess what their latest evil scheme might be. Bagley thought they'd bugged all the telephone lines. But I thought it more plausible that they'd poisoned the food, because the entire Residency staff had recently been down with gastroenteritis.

"I blame the Serbs for that," said Bagley. "They control the supply lines."

I tried again. "Photograph all the Intelligence files?"

"There's no Intelligence in the UN, don't you know that? Only Public Information and Military Information."

This was true. The UN was transparent to the point of invisibility, and in so many ways.

"Catch Lieutenant Harris in a compromising position and then blackmail her?" suggested Bagley.

"Leave Lieutenant Harris out of this."

"Why?"

"She's off limits, that's why."

"Why is she off limits?"

"Ok, I'm done with this."

Bagley went to make some irritating comment, but was interrupted by the head chef. He had two steaming mugs of coffee in his thin, sweaty hands and a grin on his face. Then a huge explosion rocked the building and he dropped the coffee on the floor.

Outside, there was mayhem. The small contingent of Danish soldiers who had responsibility for securing the Residency were running around shouting *Helmets on! Flak jackets on! Helmets on! Flak jackets on!* Dust was rising from a building close alongside the Residency, and a vehicle parked on the streets was on fire. I ran out though the security gates. Someone was on the ground screaming and medics were pulling bandages from their backpacks and someone else was unravelling an intravenous drip as Danish soldiers with guns pushed us and shoved us back towards the Residency.

I could see it was a mere boy on the ground. He was writhing in agony, and I could see that his leg had been partially severed below the knee. Two more children were being laid out on the sidewalk, their lifeless bodies covered in blood. I realised that a mortar round had exploded close to our compound, the United Nations compound, the general's headquarters and the focal point of international authority in this fucked-up city, this fucked-up country, this fucked-up situation.

I stumbled back into the Residency and up the stairs to my room. I struggled into my flak jacket and fumbled with my helmet strap and cocked my puny pistol. Then another round exploded close-by, and I heard there were French casualties; and I wondered in my panic if this meant war with the Serbs and the end of all this dicking around at checkpoints.

Then more explosions started to rock the city and thousands of bullets were tearing the place up. The Danes were trying to insist we all return to our rooms, but the officers and the staff were wanting to witness the craziness. They were standing on the Residency's balconies and straining for a better view with their flak jackets open and their combat helmets dangling from their hands.

I bumped into Lieutenant Harris and she grabbed me, held me close for a moment so I could feel her heart pounding in her chest. I could see that her eyes were on fire, alive and excited, but not at all scared.

"This is more what it used to be like," she said. "But don't worry, sweetheart. They won't target this place for directly. It will all settle down, you'll see."

Then she was gone, and I was left dazed, confused and breathless, because she'd called me sweetheart and because she'd held me close, and because bullets were still cracking over the roof of the Residency.

Then there was the deafening roar of NATO aircraft flying low over the city, unseen because of the cloud but unmistakable because of the noise. They made several passes, and then the explosions stopped and the shooting settled down; and the children's dead bodies and the wounded were whisked away in white personnel carriers marked with red crosses whilst the Danes went around banging on doors shouting *All clear! All clear! All clear!*

Then I saw the head chef encouraging me to come back into the canteen, and there was Bagley, sat calmly in our usual spot, drinking coffee and preparing to munch on hard tack biscuits thickly smeared with strawberry jam.

Within a few hours I knew from the major that the general strongly suspected the Bosnians may have been responsible for firing the mortars towards our compound, because they were small calibre bombs and could not possibly have made the distance from the nearest Serb lines. When I asked why the Muslims would do this, the major told me that they were always trying to make it appear the Serbs were the aggressors so that the United Nations or the United Kingdom or the United States or even NATO would retaliate and join the war on their side to defeat the Serbs and allow them to achieve a final victory over their enemies in alliance with the international community.

This is all way above my head. It was double-think and double-talk, and maybe the major and the general were crazy because the Serbs *were* the aggressors. This is what the Americans believed, this is what the world believed, this is what everyone in Sarajevo believed; and as far as I could make out, this is what even the BBC believed. And if the BBC believed then we should all believe, because the BBC *always* told the truth and we should always believe in that.

CHAPTER 4

Lieutenant Harris was then away for a few days, and I missed her terribly.

"You're very quiet," said Bagley as we hung around the Residency awaiting our next detail.

"I've a lot to think about."

"You're thinking about Lieutenant bloody Isabella Harris, you horny toad."

I hadn't known that her name was Isabella.

"Shut up. You don't know what you're talking about."

"I know a horn-dog when I see one," said Bagley. He blew a smoke ring and poked his finger through its hole.

"Go and service the Land Rover," I said. "That's an order."

I moped around the Residency, hoping something would come up to take my mind away from thoughts of unlikely romance and unrequited love. I didn't have to wait for long.

"We're going for a run?" I asked.

"With the Boss," said the Observers' warrant officer, a man not to be argued with. "He seems to think it might calm things down."

The general must be mad. Everyone is mad. We couldn't go for a run, there was nowhere to run. This was a war zone, people didn't go running in a war zone.

"Where are we going?" I asked.

"Past the Serb front lines." The warrant officer didn't seem to be worried by this at all. He must have been too old to care. Or maybe he had been there for too long. He had the look of a man who'd been there for too long, in any case.

"They fired mortars at us the other day," I protested. "Don't you think they might try to shoot us?"

"PT kit, main gate, ten minutes," he said. "Ready to go. You do have running gear?"

I was tempted to tell him I didn't, but he'd already gone. I tried to find Bagley, but he'd disappeared. I went to my room and pulled on my trainers and shorts. I tried to figure if I should carry a gun, but then thought that the front line would be several hundred yards away at its closest and a pistol would be useless in a firefight. I found some thin gloves and a hat because the weather was seriously chill and it would have been embarrassing to become a cold weather casualty in the heart of a war zone.

A small group of runners had gathered at the Residency's security gate. The general's bodyguard was amongst them wearing combat trousers, boots and a maroon sweat-top. He had a pistol shoved in his belt and was carrying a stabbing knife. So I thought of going back to get my own gun, but there was no time because here was the general. Then the gate was open and we were off.

The general led with the bodyguard on his shoulder and the rest of us strung out behind. We jogged steadily uphill with the park on our right, then into the suburbs and over the crest of a hill, and then down a street with locals and Bosnian soldiers looking at us as if we were out of our minds. Steam began to rise from our heads and from our shoulders as we warmed to the task.

The general was no slouch and the route was no pushover. We descended towards a large Muslim cemetery that I knew to be a regular target for snipers. Evidently the bastards found it amusing to shoot at people who were grieving over the graves of the dead. But the snipers held their fire and we cleared the open ground at the foot of the cemetery, and once again threaded our way steadily uphill through a built-up area before slipping off steeply downhill to our right and then out into full view of the Serb frontline along a track that crossed open fields.

An armoured Land Rover tagged along at our rear and the general increased the pace. A couple of bullets cracked over our heads. The bodyguard made a sweeping gesture with his arm, and the Land Rover roared up alongside the general to provide a shield from the sniper fire. We angled back towards the city. The general told the bodyguard to have the Land Rover back off, so the bodyguard swept his arm in a backwards gesture and the Land Rover slowed down to tuck-in behind us.

We ran a little further and the pace increased even more. I was sweating freely now and my lungs were on fire, but the general seemed unconcerned and the bodyguard, for all his bulk, stayed on his shoulder. I dug-in because probably the safest place to be was here, alongside the general. If the snipers tried again, at least the Land Rover would be with us in a heartbeat.

And the snipers did try again, but perhaps they were playing with us because their fire was hardly accurate and in any case the general told the bodyguard to have the Land Rover back-off. So I wondered if I should just stay with the Land Rover as it dropped back and pulled forward, because that might be safer. But the bodyguard glanced over his shoulder and glared at me, so I knew I had to stay with the general.

The sniper fire came closer. The Land Rover didn't even make it this time, because the general told the bodyguard to have the Land Rover *keep the fuck away;* and we trailed along the track like a parade of ducks on a fairground range waiting to be knocked down by a lucky shot. But nobody got hit.

Soon we were approaching the ruins of the Zetra Olympic stadium, but just as I was thinking that all was well and that shortly we'd be back at the Residency, the warrant officer grabbed my arm and spun me around and pushed me ahead of him back towards the open fields. I asked him *what are we doing, are you crazy?* and he told me that he'd dropped his radio somewhere back there and we needed to find it.

So we ran once again across the open fields and close to the Serb frontline, and I thought that this man was insane and I thought that the general was insane too. The Serbs didn't fire off a single round until we'd cleared the open fields and threaded our way back through the suburbs and were close to the open area by the cemetery. Then they let rip with a whole fusillade of rounds that smacked into the buildings in front of us. So we went to ground, and right there at his feet was the warrant officer's missing radio.

As the sniper fire tailed-off, my companion looked at me and grinned and challenged me to a sprint across the face of the cemetery with its white marble headstones and freshly dug graves. Then I knew that everyone in this city was mad, ourselves included, because we were off and running with the crack and thump of Serb sniper fire all around and our own hysterical laughter ringing in our ears.

But as we reached safety on the far side of the gap, the hard words of angry men told us they thought it was our stupid fault that some poor woman had been hit in the legs by a fusillade of high velocity bullets meant for us, that we were stupid and reckless to go running and attract all that incoming fire from across the frontline. And it was very difficult to argue against that.

So we increased our pace and made good time over the last mile and got safely back to the Residency, to find the general and the bodyguard doing sit-ups and press-ups on the oil-stained ground of its overcrowded car park, just inside the gate.

CHAPTER 5

Lieutenant Isabella Harris returned to Sarajevo, but it seemed like she was avoiding me. I began to feel that I'd imagined the connection between us, that it had been no more than a foolish infatuation; a hormonal spike, a lust-driven dream. Then one afternoon, when winter's frost was hanging heavy in the air, she poked her head into the office and declared that she needed a driver for an unusual assignment.

"Private Bagley is available," I said.

"No, I want you."

"OK."

So with the light fading and the routine sniper fire beginning to pop away across the infamous Sniper Alley down by the Holiday Inn Hotel, we drove deep into the suburbs of the city and towards an area I was wholly unfamiliar with.

The lieutenant navigated entirely from memory, and it was very clear she knew this area well. We were stopped at a Bosnian Army checkpoint and it was clear that the soldiers were puzzled why a lone United Nations vehicle was headed this way. But she fired away at them in Serbo-Croat and suddenly it was all salutes and smiles and they waved us through.

We stopped outside a small apartment block that appeared to be fully intact, one of the few buildings in this city I'd seen that didn't bear the physical scars of war.

"Keep the engine running, I'll be back in a jiffy," she said, and headed off inside. I sat and drumming my fingers on the steering wheel, wondering what we were doing here.

She emerged a few minutes later with a couple of civilians who were laughing and joking and holding each other close as they piled into the back of the vehicle.

"How do you do?" asked the man, extending his hand and smiling broadly. "My name is Mirsad, and this is my girlfriend Almira."

His English was precise, excellent.

"Nice to meet you," I said.

"Peace be upon you."

"Let's go," said the lieutenant.

Ten minutes later, we stopped outside a row of houses that were positioned high in the suburb. It was becoming quite dark by now, and far below I could see the occasional tracer round flash across the confrontation line. There were no city lights as such, and certainly no streetlights, for the Bosnians imposed both a blackout and an after-dark curfew to keep things quiet. I knew that they enforced the curfew rigidly, and was a little surprised that Mirsad and Almira seemed so relaxed to be out and about with night drawing-in fast. They must have been important people.

The Land Rover doors opened and my passengers got out. The lieutenant paused for a moment, looked at me sternly, and then smiled.

"You too. Come on."

There was music coming from one of the houses. We entered through a passageway that was draped with heavy sacking to contain the light. The rooms were filled with cigarette smoke and the music was very loud. Officers and civilians stood around in huddled groups holding conversations. Bottles of cheap wine were strewn around the place and crates of beer were piled high behind a makeshift bar in the dining room. The house was large, and perhaps once was grand. But now it was a bit like a cross between a Prohibition speakeasy and a Soho jazz club.

"Isn't this *fun?*" The lieutenant had me by the arm and was navigating us around the various clusters of debate. She grabbed a half-full bottle of wine, took a slug and then offered it to me.

"Are you sure?" I asked.

"Why not?" she said. "Night off!"

We cycled through the crowd, and I soon realised that many of the civilians were either journalists or civil servants from the Bosnian Government. Most of the chatter was in English so it wasn't hard for me to follow, and I was grateful for that. There was much talk about the possibility of America coming into the war and much derision about the United Nations.

"The UN is like a tampon," I heard one local saying. "It just sits there stuck in a hole; absorbing, swelling, blocking the path to victory. It should withdraw, let things flow."

The lieutenant latched-on to some young captain and disappeared, so I hung around the edge of this conversation.

"Let the Serbs come into town? It would be a massacre," said a squat, middle-aged man whom I vaguely recognised from the television.

"We can put up with a bit more suffering," said the local. "It might be just the thing to shake up this stalemate, get the international community properly engaged."

"Oh come on. If the world hasn't jumped in by now, it never will," said the television man.

"But if we see a bit more blood on the streets, a few more marketplace bombings? You journo's love that. You'll splash it all over Sky and CNN. Then even D.C. will have to pay attention."

"Look, the Yanks have no interest whatsoever in this place. And anyway, is that your President's policy? Allow the Serbs to kill even more of your people?"

"I don't think…" The local paused and looked at me. "I'm sorry, have we met?" he asked, glancing at the corporal's chevrons on my shoulder. He seemed to be displeased with the intrusion, and was probably wondering what the hell a low-life like me was doing in this place. I began to mumble an excuse, when suddenly Mirsad was at my side, all smiles and charm, shaking hands and offering more wine.

"This man is with me and he works in the Residency. He's a friend of Bella's."

Then everything was fine, because evidently the lieutenant was something of a celebrity amongst these people and I had learned that her friends called her Bella.

So I found myself swept into the conversation and learned that the journalists were very smart, and that Bosnian Government Ministers – because the local man who wanted the Serbs to kill more of his fellow Muslims was indeed a Bosnian Government Minister - were even smarter. I tried not to say much, because these people were immersed in the politics whereas I was just a low-ranking nobody. But it was fascinating and frightful and dizzying all at the same time.

After a while I felt another tug at my elbow and it was Lieutenant Bella Harris, a little bit tipsy, but clearly enjoying herself. She began to say something, but suddenly all the lights went out and there was total darkness apart from the burning tips of a dozen or more cigarettes; then raucous laughter and stumbling and falling as a couple of flashlights came on.

People who knew their way around the place began to light candles. I could hear gunfire close-by and realised that locals were taking potshots in the general direction of the house. They must have become annoyed at the noise of the music, or perhaps jealous of the partying. But they were uncertain where to aim because the blackout drapes had been so effectively hung.

The lieutenant was clinging to me tightly, so I chanced an arm around her waist and knew I was a little bit drunk. But then so was she, and she didn't resist. Then her tiny, cool hand was on the back of my neck and she was on tiptoe, pulling me down and kissing me full on the lips. Her tongue was soft and moist and warm, and for a breathless moment I held her close.

Then all at once the electric light came back on, the music started playing again and the lieutenant was moving away, demure and disengaged. She finished the dregs of her wine, shot me an up-from-under look with those amazing grey eyes, and then disappeared back into the crowd.

Driving downhill in the Land Rover, Mirsad and Almira were talking animatedly between themselves about the political situation, but all I could think of was the curve of the lieutenant's waist and the warmth of her thigh against mine.

Then Almira thrust her head forward and asked me drunkenly what I thought of the situation and whether the general felt he could persuade the Americans to intervene; and how was he handling the Head of Civil Affairs at the Residency, who was from Russia and was a very close friend of

President Yeltsin, didn't I know? And didn't I know that the Russians had been arming and supporting the Serbs because they too were of the Orthodox faith, and what did I think about that?

I replied that the whole situation was a tragedy, that Sarajevo was a beautiful city being fought over and destroyed in the name of religion and race, and that I couldn't possibly talk about what was happening in the general's headquarters because I was responsible to a chain of command and there could be serious consequences if I gave away sensitive information. Then the lieutenant's hand was on my thigh, squeezing reassuringly, knowing that her friend was smart and that I was just a baby in this game.

But Almira continued, telling me not to be naïve, that I wore the blue beret of the United Nations, and that me and the general and the whole corrupt set-up down at the Residency and at the UN headquarters in Zagreb were all part of the problem; that when the Americans did finally come into the war on the side of the Muslim people the Serbs would all be destroyed, and that every one of them and all their families would be made to pay with their blood. Because this was the Will of Allah and this was the destiny of the Bosniak Muslim race.

I was shocked by her words. Shocked that a woman of so much beauty and grace could carry such thoughts in her mind and feel such uncompromising hatred in her heart.

Mirsad reached through the driver's window as Almira disappeared into the apartment block. "You must forgive my girlfriend's intensity," he said. "She lost her parents in in an artillery attack, you know. She has very strong views."

I could see this would make her bitter, after all.

"But she is right in saying that the Serbs will pay," he added. "Goodbye, young man. I hope to see you again sometime."

We drove away and I thought about stopping the Land Rover somewhere quiet, but the lieutenant seemed subdued and thoughtful. I asked her what she thought of her friends.

"Oh, they're alright. Almira's parents were very nice people. It was tragic they were killed."

"You knew them?"

"We were very close."

"You know a lot of people here."

"I do."

We were close to the Residency when she asked me to pull over. I could feel my heart beginning to race and my blood pressure rising. She turned to face me and reached for my hands. I could see in the pale moonlight that she had tears in her eyes.

"Back there… when I kissed you…" she paused.

"Yes?"

"You mustn't think…"

"Think what?"

"That we can make anything of this."

"Why not?" Her hands were shaking a little and I tried to reach for her, but she pulled back. "Come on Bella… I can call you Bella can't I?"

She nodded.

"You know there's a connection," I said. "You wouldn't be teasing me otherwise."

"Officers can't have relations with enlisted ranks."

"Surely you don't believe that old crap? Not in this place?"

"Those are the rules."

"To hell with the rules."

"Well, we're not making love here," she said.

And then I knew that we *would* make love, even if it wasn't to be here, this very night, amongst the oil and grease and ration packs and snow shovels crammed into the back of this rancid old truck.

"Where then?"

"Oh, we'll figure it," she said. "But you mustn't call me Bella in front of the general, or any of the other staff."

"Not even in front of Bagley?"

She laughed, and then her tears were gone. "Especially not in front of Private Bagley."

We drove into the compound and parked-up, wished each other goodnight, then went our separate ways. I found it very hard to sleep, and wondered why she was crying.

CHAPTER 6

Bagley and I were kept busy enough over the following days and weeks, driving around the city on various tasks both menial and meaningful. Sometimes the French were harder to deal with than the warring factions, particularly at their checkpoints around the airport. They were under strict orders to prevent UN personnel moving through dangerous areas in anything other than armoured vehicles. We managed to convince them that the Land Rover's soft canvas shell was a new form of bulletproof material that was impervious to small arms fire. They were both deceived and impressed.

One evening Lieutenant Harris and the major had me drive them to a narrow, bullet-scarred street close to Sniper Alley. The lieutenant jumped out as soon as we stopped and spoke with a burly character stood outside the entrance of a bar. I saw her press some notes into his hand, and he nodded. The major was already in through the door as she came back to the vehicle.

"Don't worry about the Land Rover," she said. "That guy will keep an eye on it."

The place was thick with smoke and music and laughter. A girl was sat on a stool at one end of the room, strumming her guitar and singing through a coarse PA system. Off-duty soldiers from the Bosnian army were clustered in groups, their uniforms filthy, faces unshaven, eyes deep-set and bloodshot.

People were clapping and drinking and talking loudly to make themselves heard, and then the major was handing a large glass of wine to the lieutenant and looking at me as if I had two heads. But Lieutenant Harris explained what she had arranged for the vehicle's security, so he shrugged his shoulders, handed me his glass of wine and forced his way back to the bar to order more.

"Super place, eh?" The lieutenant was pressed up hard against me, standing on tiptoe so her mouth was close to my ear. "A lot of these people are journo's."

I took a look around. Some faces did look familiar.

"Same crowd as before?"

"Some of them. They're in and out. Here today, Rwanda tomorrow. Chasing the latest atrocity."

The major rejoined us, carrying a fresh bottle of red. He topped up our glasses, looking at the pair of us with narrowed eyes.

"Lovebirds, or just friends?" he asked.

I felt myself blush, a greedy child caught with his hands in the sweetie jar. But the major let loose a terrific guffaw and said, "Who cares? It's a bloody war zone!" He spun away and merged into the crowd, and suddenly I liked him a lot.

Lieutenant Harris was laughing and I tried to pull her close, but she pushed me firmly away. "Circulate. Have fun. See you later." And then she too, was gone.

I fell into conversation with a balding man of indeterminate age who was a little drunk.

"Never thought I'd see so many goddam Muslims drinking booze," he said.

"You're an American?"

"You can tell by my accent, huh?"

"It's an indicator."

He offered me a thin cigar, which I accepted.

"Journalist?" I asked.

He nodded, and we lit up.

"Soldier?" he asked.

"You can tell by my uniform?"

"It's an indicator."

We both laughed, and blew smoke.

"Been here long?" he asked.

"A couple of months."

"Must have seen some things."

"Some."

"Goddam Serbs."

"I suppose so."

"We should blow those motherfuckers off the face of the earth," he said. "Goddam UN is useless. No offence."

"We deliver humanitarian relief," I said.

"Only when the goddam Serbs let you," growled the American. "Why don't you guys just shoot your way through the checkpoints?"

"Because we don't want a war with the Serbs."

"Why not? Their snipers are killing kids, for Chrissake!"

"We're neither equipped nor mandated for it," I said, reasonably.

"So tell me this, Mr United Nations soldier; how do you feel when you speak with those fuckers at their checkpoints?"

"How do *you* feel when you speak with them?" I asked.

"Speak with them? I don't speak with them. Why would I speak with them?" He looked surprised.

"For balance, maybe? You are a journalist, after all."

"Balance? They're goddam Nazis for fuck's sake! Where's the sense in speaking with Nazis?"

"Thanks for the cigar," I said.

"You're welcome." He staggered away in a haze of blue smoke, muttering to himself.

I was glad the interview was over.

Somebody tapped me on the shoulder. It was Almira, the woman from the apartment block.

"Hi there! I recognise you from the party." She too was a little drunk, but her smile was stunning and she pecked me on the cheek. "Are you here with Bella?"

"Yes, she's circulating."

"Ah yes, circulating. Gathering intelligence. Spreading disinformation." She tapped her nose. "She's very good at what she does."

I wondered what it was that Bella did.

"I heard you were up on Mount Igman, with the French," Almira continued, wrapping a slender arm around my shoulders. "Tell me all about it. Was it exciting?"

"Not exactly. A little frightening, really. Who told you I was there?"

"See, you should neither confirm nor deny. You are no spy. Now I *know* you were there."

I offered her some wine, and she drank it straight from the bottle. The noise in the bar was louder than ever. The soldiers were singing along with the girl on the stool. I asked Almira to tell me about the song.

"It's a song about life and death," she said. "And victory."

Then she joined in, waving the wine bottle in the air, swaying in time with the music. I wondered how I could get away, find the lieutenant, get out of this place. But Almira had me tightly by the arm and some of the soldiers were looking at me with that thousand-yard stare. So I pretended to be impressed, and swayed along with her. I looked around and could see that some of the journalists had tears in their eyes. The whole scene could have been lifted straight from any underground bar in occupied Paris or a beer cellar in triumphant Berlin during the early 1940's.

The song finished to rapturous applause, and Almira asked me once again to tell her about Mount Igman.

"We saw hundreds of Bosnian soldiers coming down the road," I said. "They'd mounted a commando raid against the Serbs, killed a bunch of their medics in a command post. Caught them off-guard."

"So brave! It was the Black Swans, you know. They're the best."

"The Black Swans?" I asked.

"Special Forces. They're quite ruthless. Did you see them?"

"I don't know. I saw many soldiers. It was dark."

"They wear black uniforms, and bandanas. You know, headscarves. Like Rambo."

"Then I did see some of them," I said. "They looked exhausted."

"You did?" She was quivering with excitement. "Oh, you're so lucky! Those boys are my heroes."

I thought of captured women having their throats cut and captured men being burned alive, and I realised in that moment there was a gulf of morality that separated such people from the men and women of the United Nations Protection Force.

"Their families must be very proud," I said.

"Oh, you have no idea."

No, I didn't suppose I did.

The air outside the bar seemed crystal clear, and I took deep breaths to cleanse the smoke from my lungs. People were spilling onto the street, laughing and singing. Lieutenant Harris and the major were waiting by the Land Rover. They were engaged in urgent conversation. I could see that something was afoot, but they clammed up when they saw me and we drove to the Residency in silence. I parked the vehicle and they disappeared towards the office. I headed for my bunk and drank two litres of water in the hope of minimizing the inevitable hangover.

A few minutes later there was a banging on the door that startled me but didn't make the recumbent Bagley even twitch. It was Lieutenant Harris.

"Office. Now."

The major was sat on the edge of his small desk with a strained look on his face, and I felt I must be in trouble. The lieutenant closed the door and sat herself down, looking at me thoughtfully.

"OK," said the major. "Here's the deal. We have a job to do tomorrow evening that you can help with, but it could be a bit dicey. Left of field, so to speak, not what you're used to."

"You can say no if you're not up for it," said the lieutenant.

"Tell me," I said.

So he informed me that for some months now the Observers had been smuggling civilians through the lines of confrontation, repatriating Serbs who had been stranded in Muslim Sarajevo with their people on the other side, and smuggling Muslims in the opposite direction.

It was an unauthorized operation being conducted for purely humanitarian reasons, he said. No strategic significance, no tactical gain; nothing to do with the UN's mission and no prospect of reward or recognition. Just something that the Observers had developed themselves, a sideline that gave everyone involved a kick, an invisible stiff finger to the warring factions on all sides of the divide.

I asked how successful the operation had been, and exactly what he wanted me to do. So he told me that every mission to date had been successful, that I needed to be aware that the implications of failure could be catastrophic for everyone involved, and that all I needed to do was drive an advance vehicle through various military checkpoints to ensure that the road ahead was clear for the team bringing the family through.

So I asked who the family was and he told me it was an old Serb couple who'd been hiding in the city for almost two years, and that if found they'd be beaten, tortured and executed; and that if they were found in our vehicles they'd be dragged out and shot at the side of the road.

So I asked what we would do if they were found in our vehicles and he told me that each of us had to make our own decision on that, but he had always known that in those circumstances he personally would do everything in his power to protect them, including shooting people dead if necessary.

So I said I would be delighted to be part of the team, Sir; and he jumped up and clapped me on the shoulder and said that Bella would sort out the details and that I was a good man, but not to call him Sir.

I returned to my room and wondered what kind of major he was, and what he would like me to call him instead. Then I fell asleep with all my clothes on, too much wine in my belly and the taste of stale cigars rank in my mouth.

CHAPTER 7

The next day, there were members of the major's team everywhere. I was still nursing a hangover even though by then it was early evening, but I was caught up in the excitement as the launch of the repatriation mission drew close. Everyone crowded into our tiny office, the major provided a clear and concise briefing, and then we deployed to the neighbourhood where the old Serb couple were hiding.

I knew by now that these operations were usually run as a blind call that involved a knock on the door, a letter from a close family member living on the other side of the confrontation lines being thrust into the target's hands, a terse instruction from the major that they had just fifteen minutes to prepare and that this was their only chance to get out of the city; then into a vehicle without any luggage and away if they agreed to come. Some of course refused, because they would be surrendering their lives into the major's hands and this could be a trap. No target was ever provided a second opportunity.

But in this case, the old couple was well known to Lieutenant Harris and the major. They were well prepared, though a little confused.

Lieutenant Harris instructed me to park our Land Rover in an adjoining street and await further instructions. We were wearing civilian clothes. Our combat jackets and our blue United Nations berets were ready in the vehicle, to be used as we drove through the checkpoints. She left me listening on a radio that was hidden under my coat. I was using an earpiece and could hear other members of the operation checking-in with our office. Someone was repeating back all transmissions for the sake of clarity.

The night was foggy, which was an advantage. I knew that a Bosnian Army security post was positioned a short distance along the road. The major reported that he was in position, and that the old couple was ready. Then they were being moved down the stairs.

Suddenly the lieutenant was on the radio, urgently calling for me to join her opposite the apartment entrance. I got out of the Land Rover and walked nervously along the pavement, every step louder than was reasonable, every moment expecting a member of the Bosnian security police to step out of the shadows and confront me. Then I was with her, and she pulled me into a doorway. I could see soldiers at the security post ahead of us standing around and talking, rifles slung over their shoulders, breath condensing on the night air.

"Timing has to be perfect," she said. "We'll call it from here."

"Why do you need me?"

"Because a man and a woman in a doorway are less suspicious than someone waiting alone." She sounded very nervous.

The major was in position at the apartment entrance. One of our vehicles was approaching. The lieutenant counted it down, two hundred metres, one hundred, fifty… then she called an abort on the radio, and the vehicle continued past and disappeared around a corner because the soldiers at the checkpoint were looking at it and there was no way we could get the old couple onboard without them being seen.

"Bugger," exclaimed the lieutenant. "We need a deception." She sounded even more nervous, but in the pale light I could see that her lips were thin-set and determined. She instructed me to stay where I was, and to call the major's vehicle forward when the Bosnian soldiers were looking the other way. Then she stepped out of the doorway, walked quickly up the road to the security post and engaged the soldiers in conversation.

I called the major's vehicle around again, counting it down towards the apartment entrance. Lieutenant Harris had the full attention of the Bosnian soldiers. She was alone and they were crowding around, touching her, pulling at her clothes, questioning her. The vehicle came to a halt. Shadowy figures bundled the old couple into the back. The lieutenant fell to the ground but got up again, and I could have sworn she reached up and kissed one of the soldiers on his mouth. Then the major's vehicle was mobile and the lieutenant's voice was on the radio, breathless and anxious, calling for me to pick her up on the main road as quickly as I could.

I drove along the street and past the security post, but there was no sign of her. Four or five soldiers were smoking and laughing between themselves, sharing some kind of joke. My heart was racing, but then there she was, up on the main road, waiting at a tram stop. Which was ridiculous, because the trams weren't running. I pulled up and she jumped in. Her hair was dishevelled, and I could see that her hands were shaking.

"Go!" she said, and we drove towards the first of the confrontation line checkpoints.

"What did you do?"

"Told them I was a hooker," she said. "Promised I'd bring some of my friends to take care of them."

"Are you insane?"

"Probably. Pull over, we have to get our uniforms on."

A moment later and we were mobile again. I glanced at the lieutenant.

"You OK?"

"Don't worry, I'll be fine." She lit a cigarette. I could see that her hands were shaking and that tears were coursing down her cheeks.

"Back there…"

"They're just animals," she said. "It's OK."

"Are you sure?"

"I'm sure. I just wish this was over."

I could see the glow of coal burning in a brazier ahead of us. Isabella began to provide a running commentary on our progress over the radio. I knew by now that the major's vehicle would be following at a discreet distance, ready to peel off and return the old couple to their apartment if security was too tight at the checkpoint.

But security couldn't have been looser. The barrier had been locked-off in a lifted position and the soldiers were clustered around the brazier, smoking and talking, warming their hands over the fire. They didn't even glance up as we drove through. Moments later we heard that the major's vehicle was safely through behind us. Then we were in no-man's land with the fog closing-in, enveloping us in a dense cloud that reflected our yellow sidelights.

We slowed down to walking pace, weaving from one side of the road to the other because the fog was so thick. White tape marking the presence of minefields appeared at the edge of the tarmac. I knew that to left and right there would be shattered buildings, their ghostly remains pockmarked with thousands of bullet strikes. This was the frontline of battle, a First World War landscape where the ground had been churned into a quagmire by relentless artillery fire and where heavily fortified trenches zigzagged their way across the fields.

Somebody fired off an illumination flare, which popped high above us and turned the fog bright pink; then another and another, in quick succession.

"This isn't good, it isn't good!" said the lieutenant.

I could feel hackles rising on the nape of my neck. The saliva dried in my mouth and I braced myself for a hail of incoming bullets.

The flares drifted down. The pink light faded and then died. We continued to weave our way forward.

"They're just checking us out," I said. My voice was pinched, and I realised the major had been quite correct. This wasn't the kind of thing I was used to at all.

The Serbs were more diligent when we reached their checkpoint. But the lieutenant spoke to them quietly, urgently, and after calling ahead on a field telephone they lifted their barrier and waved us through.

"We're safe now," said Lieutenant Harris. "They were expecting us."

We reached our drop-off point, and a few minutes later the major's vehicle arrived with its precious cargo. I helped offload the old couple. They were very confused and a little anxious. The place was deserted, but we found them a room and managed to get a small electric heater going to warm them. A Serb military liaison officer arrived. He seemed annoyed at the inconvenience of it all.

We settled down for a cold night, warmed at least by the certain knowledge that the old couple's lives would no longer be hanging by a fine thread in the heart of wartime Sarajevo. I tried to engage Isabella in conversation, but she seemed distant and preoccupied. I watched her nervously smoke several cigarettes, and as I drifted into a fitful sleep she was sat very upright on a hard chair staring at a blank wall.

The following morning the Serb liaison officer was more affable and we eat a frugal breakfast washed down with lukewarm coffee. The old couple were spirited away and I never saw them again.

We travelled back to the city in convoy and were stopped by both the French and the Bosnians, who wanted to know why we spent a whole night on the Serb side of the confrontation line. But the major and the lieutenant evidently had some plausible explanation, because after a short delay in each case we were allowed to proceed.

Back at the Residency the major thanked me for my help, then told me that he and I would be travelling alone to the Muslim enclave of Žepa the next day and that I'd better get some rest because it would be a long journey. I tried to track down the lieutenant, but she had disappeared. So I went to find Bagley but he was out on a detail. I serviced the Land Rover, packed my kit for the following day, then crashed onto my bunk and fell quickly into a dreamless sleep.

CHAPTER 8

Early the following morning we set out for the isolated Muslim pocket of Žepa some sixty kilometres east of Sarajevo. The major told me that we had been directed by the general to check out the status of the Ukrainian Detachment, a company formation of UN soldiers tasked with defending this enclave. They had not been heard from for almost three weeks.

We made rapid progress out of the city but were then stopped and searched at a Serb checkpoint located in Rogatica, a town midway between Sarajevo and our destination. The checkpoint was manned by a rough looking bunch of militia dressed in a mixture of combat fatigues and jeans. They were heavily armed and unshaven, hard-nosed and very much in control.

We were ordered out of our vehicle. They systematically searched its interior, then opened our backpacks and spread their contents along the edge of the road. I kept hold of my rifle, trying to appear indifferent and at ease, but clutching it a little too tightly.

"Why so much gasoil?" they asked.

We were carrying a couple of cans filled with diesel because the return journey was too far to cover on a single tank of fuel.

"So we can get back to Sarajevo from Žepa," said the major.

The checkpoint commander, an older man with a thick mop of grey hair and a hand-rolled cigarette hanging from the corner of his mouth, laughed and said something in Serbo-Croat to his men. They also laughed, and three of them cocked their weapons.

"It is against the rules," said the commander. "We will have to confiscate this. You cannot take gasoil to the Muslims. It is contraband."

The cans were taken away and returned to us an hour later, empty. By now the search had been completed and no further contraband found. We were free to go.

Some distance later we hit a patch of ice on a curving mountain road. The Land Rover almost slid over the edge and into a river far below. We fixed snow chains to all four tires and continued with the major now driving. The day was wearing on and we were traveling very slowly because the road was heavily rutted under the snow.

Eventually we reached a contingent of Polish troops manning a heavily sandbagged UN roadblock. I noticed that several of the sandbags had bullet holes in them. The Poles looked nervous and stressed. We learned that they regularly came under sniper fire from the Serbs, though when I checked my compass it seemed more likely that the bullets had been fired from the direction of a thin tree line bordering the Žepa salient.

They raised the barrier and we drove onwards through a long stretch of no-man's land until we were close to the trees. Then there was a Bosnian checkpoint staffed by thin men with suspicious eyes who checked our papers and rummaged in the back of our vehicle. They seemed disappointed that we were carrying nothing, not even spare rations because that too would have been considered contraband by the Serbs and could have got us arrested.

Then they raised their barrier and we began to descend along a broad, twisting track through thick woods towards the town of Žepa far below, a town that we could vaguely make out in the dwindling light and through a frost-laden fog that was rising from the valley floor.

On the track we passed several large carts hauled by skinny oxen and filled with hand-felled logs. I realised that the fog must in part have been caused by the smoke from burning fires. So I thought that the people of Žepa must be warm, because they were surrounded by a forest that could provide an almost limitless supply of fuel. And I thought that they must have food because the oxen had not been eaten, and that there may be some truth in the rumour that the Americans had been parachuting supplies into these Muslim pockets to save the people from being starved.

And I thought that if this was indeed the case, then *good for them* because we knew for sure that the United Nations convoys rarely got through, either here in Žepa or to Goražde in the south or to Srebrenica in the north, or to Bihać in the west; or even to Tuzla in the far north, though at least there they had an airfield that was under United Nations control. When convoys did get through they had often been looted on the way. Or, if it was a civilian convoy with no UN escort, it could be diverted just before it arrived to be looted; and sometimes the drivers were shot dead, even if they were working with a charity.

By the time we reached the bottom of the track we could see that dozens of people were waiting to greet us, many carrying flaming torches to see by. Men, women and children, dressed warmly enough for sure, but all of them bearing sallow complexions and hollow eyes; people who were dog-tired and short on hope, anticipating much yet expecting little.

Two large men stepped from the crowd, one carrying a rifle crooked in his arm, the other with a pitchfork balanced on his shoulder. The major stepped out of the Land Rover and offered his hand, which was ignored. The crowd shuffled forward, glancing into the back of our vehicle and looked up towards the track we'd just descended.

"Where is the rest of the convoy?" asked the man with the rifle.

"There is no convoy," said the major.

"See, I told you," said the man with the pitchfork, then shouted something to the crowd in Serbo-Croat. There was a loud, collective moan, and the people began to disperse.

"Why are you here?" asked the man.

"To liaise with the Ukrainians," replied the major.

"Those crooks." The man with the gun spat on the ground. "You'll find them up at the big house."

The man with the pitchfork held me in an accusing stare, then turned abruptly and strode off into the night.

"Do you have any diesel?" asked the major.

"You can try the Ukrainians," said the man with the gun. "Though they have probably sold all theirs."

We drove up to a big white house that had a satellite television dish on its roof and a group of white armoured vehicles parked outside. We found that the Ukrainians had of course sold all of their diesel, that this is why they'd failed to communicate for so long. They had no fuel for their generators, so no power to charge their radio batteries.

We wondered what to do. We hadn't brought a radio of our own because these were also listed by the Serbs as contraband. And we had insufficient fuel to get ourselves out of here and back to Sarajevo.

The temperature was dropping and the Ukrainians were inhospitable. There was no place in town to stay, and the back of the Land Rover promised to be a frigid shelter for the night.

A teenage boy introduced himself in perfect English and offered to find us accommodation. So we accepted, and ten minutes later were spreading out our sleeping bags gratefully in a rancid barn that was marginally heated by the steaming bodies of a half dozen pathetically thin cows crapping on the floor and chewing on their cud.

The boy was back soon after first light carrying a flask of *ersatz* coffee sweetened with condensed milk. We learned that his name was Adnan, that he was the son of a sergeant in the Bosnian Army whom he hadn't seen for more than two years, and that the rest of his family lived in a small farm overlooking the River Drina close to the enclave's eastern border. He also told us that he knew where to purchase diesel fuel, though the price would be very high.

In a heartbeat the major decided that we must visit the boy's family and take a look across the Drina, though I had no idea why.

We drove as far as the roads allowed, then continued on foot at a ridiculously fast pace. But this was fine by me because the air was cold and the sooner we got done with the sightseeing the sooner we could start heading back towards Sarajevo.

We climbed steadily along a snow covered track for a couple of kilometres, then Adnan pointed directly uphill and we struck out across country, sweating with the exertion and panting as we became increasingly challenged by altitude.

After another kilometre or so our guide let us know with a casual air that this whole area was thickly sown with anti-personnel landmines, and that a neighbour had been recently blown-up by one of them. I walked more gingerly for a few minutes thereafter, but there was no let-up in the pace by the major or the boy. So caution was cast aside for the sake of pride and I managed to catch up.

We crested the hill and found ourselves on a flat plateau that had been cleared for farming. Trees clustered thickly on either side, and the plateau was interspersed with rocky escarpments. Birds were wheeling high in the sky and the sun broke through the clouds, bathing the whole scene in a glorious light. I thought to myself that the place was really pretty and wonderfully peaceful and it seemed hard to link this idyllic landscape with the horrors of the Balkans War.

Then there was a farmhouse in front of us and our guide began to whistle loudly. He ran ahead while the major and I slowed down a little to catch our breath and prepare to meet his family.

Adnan's grandparents and mother were charming hosts, though they didn't speak a word of English. The boy translated for us, and we learned that they'd managed to stay up here in their home since their son left for Sarajevo. They'd last heard from him a year ago and they didn't know if he'd survived the fighting. We undertook to try and find him when we got back to the city. The major handed a pen and notebook to Adnan's mother so she could write a letter to her husband.

The farmhouse was neatly furnished, rustic and charming. Chopped wood was piled by the hearth and water in a heavy iron pot bubbled over a blazing fire. A Madonna was hung on one of the walls, which I thought to be strange for a Muslim house. But it was a fine work of art, although the glass was cracked and dirty. Adnan's grandparents busied themselves making tea and presently their grandson reappeared with a girl in her early teens.

"This is my sister, Katarina. She understands English, but is too shy to speak."

The girl stood there, shivering from the cold; demure, blond and *petite,* her complexion flawless and her eyes a vivid shade of green. I had never seen anyone so beautiful or so vulnerable, or so pale.

We spent the rest of the morning chatting with Adnan, and learned that his grandfather had fought during the Second World War. I got the impression that the old boy was something of a hero, for he pulled out a faded black and white photograph showing himself as a young man in full military uniform. His wife fussed around us, serving slices of dried venison with soda bread and goat's cheese followed by hot tea and fresh apple juice.

But my eyes drifted back time and again to green-eyed Katarina, who sat quietly in a corner darning holes in a woollen sweater and saying nothing.

The day wore on and it became apparent that we'd be staying the night, for the grandmother had been plumping a couple of feather mattresses and unfolding thick horsehair blankets.

"You are our guests," said Adnan. "My grandmother says you must stay because it will be lucky for us, and that if you take breakfast before leaving then you will never forget, and that one day you will return."

The major was fine with this, and said we would scout the Drina tomorrow before returning to the town. Adnan assured us once again that he could find enough fuel for the Land Rover, and as the sun went down we realised that sleep must come early because there was no electricity for the light bulbs and no oil for the lamps. Katarina scurried off as soon as she could. I hoped that we'd get to see her in the morning before we departed.

Cocks were crowing before dawn, and soon after daylight we were being served fresh eggs, soda bread and more tea. Adnan's mother was helping now. Her sleeves were rolled up and I couldn't help noticing that she had long black hair on her forearms like that of a man. She also had facial hair, and when Adnan saw me staring at this he explained that it was because all the women took two or even three contraceptive pills a day to ensure they wouldn't bear a child.

"My mother isn't having an affair," he said. "We know that if the Serbs come here the women will probably be raped. And none of them wants to become pregnant like that."

I was shocked, but asked where they managed to get the contraceptives from. Adnan told me they were sold by the Ukrainians and the local crime bosses, along with tinned food and other things. When I ask where *they* got these things from, he said it was from the parachute resupplies flown in from Saudi Arabia and Egypt. I relayed this to the major and his eyes opened wide, and he said that this was valuable information but that I mustn't tell anyone else.

When Katarina appeared I could see in the brighter light of early morning that she had long, wispy hair on her upper lip and on her arms. So I thought that she too, despite her tender years, must be taking contraceptives because her family were scared for her. By now she had lost her initial shyness, and asked me where I lived in England.

"I live wherever the Army sends me, but I was born in London. That's where my family lives."

"I want to come to England," she said. "I want to study, to become a doctor. My father lived there for a while, before I was born. He says it's a wonderful place and that English people are very nice."

"It's OK. Not everyone is nice though. But you will do very well there. You must come. When all this is over."

She smiled, and her face was simply radiant.

"Yes," she said. "I will come. And maybe I will be able to see you again."

"Maybe."

"You're the first Englishman I ever met. You're nice. And you're very handsome."

I laughed, and she laughed too, shyly.

"Where do you go to school?" I asked.

"There is no school, not for a long time. My mother teaches me here. It is safer. She is very good."

"She's a very nice person."

"Yes. But she misses my father. He has been gone for such a long time." A cloud passed across her face.

It must be very tough, I thought, for such a young girl to be wondering if her father was dead or alive.

"We will find your father," I said. "I will say hello for you, give him a hug if you like."

She smiled, then leaned forward and kissed me lightly on the cheek. "That would be very nice of you," she said.

We finished our breakfast, but when we opened the door snow was falling so heavy we could barely make out the fence at the end of the garden.

"Could be in for the day," said the major.

So we closed the door again and sat around the fire and drank more thin coffee and finished off the soda bread. I wondered if the Land Rover would by now be completely buried by snow down in the valley.

There was no let-up in the weather by midday, so the major decided that we'd stay in this isolated place for a second night because by now there would be no time to make it out of the Žepa valley, even if we could make it down the track to our vehicle.

The snow blanketed everything, and peering from the cracked windows I could see that the land had taken on a shapeless form of monotone grey. The air itself was stifled and silent. Time seemed to slow down, as if caught in a gently spinning cloud of cotton wool.

The young girl stayed with us throughout the afternoon, asking questions about Sarajevo and England, her shyness completely gone, her eyes bright, intelligent and alive. Her tiny hands were fragile and thin, her nails cracked and dirty. But she had an elegance about her that reminded me of a ballerina, or a fine porcelain doll.

One moment she would be sewing something; the next, she would be using small pieces of charcoal taken from the edges of the fireplace to draw pictures of horses or cats on clean sheets of paper that her brother had, surprisingly, produced from the depths of his backpack.

"You're good at drawing," I said.

"My papa taught me," she said. "He studied art at university before he joined the Army."

"He was a good teacher."

She nodded, furrowing her brow in concentration and leaning over her sketch. "I would like to study art," she said. "But I don't want to join the Army."

"No. You shouldn't join the Army," I said.

Late in the afternoon the wind picked up, and the snow began to drift against the sides of the farmhouse. It piled up against the windows and soon all daylight was blocked out, giving the impression that we were living in a fairytale cave. Condensation ran freely down the walls, and every half hour or so our hosts would crack open a flap at the top of the front door and poke a stick through the drifted snow to ventilate the place.

We slept intermittently, ate stew that was as thin as the coffee, then fell into deeper sleep as the oil lamps burned-down and the dark of night closed-in.

I awoke the next morning with young Katarina curled up in a ball beside me on the floor, covered in a rug and hugging a sad pillow. Her grandparents were fussing around, scraping together a breakfast and brushing together snow that had blown-in under the door. We washed in freezing water poured into an aluminium pail, drying our faces on rough towels that had been torn in two to make them go further.

It took some effort to force the door open against the encroaching snow, but outside the sky was blue and the air crisp. Away from the farmhouse the snow was not so deep, and it had a solid crust that gave way to a softer underbelly every five steps or so.

"Thank you for coming to see us," said Katarina. "I hope you come back one day."

"Hey, you're coming to see us in England, remember?" I said.

She nodded, but she did look uncertain and a little sad.

We left the farmhouse mid-morning, striking out towards a distant escarpment and leaving the family waving us farewell. Katarina stayed at the door, but then suddenly shouted and came stumbling through the snow. She reached us, her breath condensing in the air and her beautiful eyes shining bright.

"I forgot... you must also give this to my father. And tell him that his little princess loves him."

She pressed a small necklace into my hand, and then she was gone. I kept looking back until we passed into dead ground and I could see her no more. Then I glanced down at the necklace. It was a small silver cross, hung from a fine silver chain.

The River Drina, far below, was fast flowing and emerald green. Tree-covered cliffs rose steeply on either side as it cut its way through a long gorge which turned sharply around the side of a large mountain some distance to our south.

"The Serbs are on the other side of the river," said Adnan. "They fire artillery rounds or mortar shells across from time to time, especially at the villages lower down. But we are quite safe up here unless someone spots us."

The place was sublimely beautiful, but we didn't linger. Adnan led us along a path through the forest. We descended along this to the track and reclaimed our Land Rover, which was only partially buried by snow. It started first time and nothing had been stolen from it.

Our young guide had us stop at a farm on the way back towards the town. An old woman with a wide smile but few teeth filled our fuel tank from a large white-painted oil drum that had UN stencilled on its side, and then insisted on also filling our spare cans even though we didn't need the extra diesel.

Adnan jumped out at the exact spot where we'd first met him. The major gave him some money, then the boy wished us a safe journey back to Sarajevo and shook our hands enthusiastically.

"Don't forget to deliver my mother's letter," he cried. "And tell my papa we miss him."

CHAPTER 9

We reached Rogatica mid-afternoon and found ourselves stuck behind a small UN convoy headed back to Sarajevo. The convoy was being denied free passage by the Serbs. The major made his way on foot to the front of the queue and returned an hour later. "Bastards won't budge an inch," he said. "Looks like we may be here for a while."

All the trucks in the convoy appeared to be empty. The drivers were predominantly British, a curious mix of military and civilian, but mainly civilian. Everyone seemed to be pretty sanguine about the situation, which I felt was not unfamiliar in their experience. I talked with some of them. We played cards, told jokes and brewed tea on hexamine stoves, whilst the Serb militia stared at us with sullen faces and local civilians asked for cigarettes or chocolate, or anything else that we were prepared to give them. Then the major suggested we top-up the Land Rover from the spare cans otherwise the Serbs would probably just confiscate the diesel again.

The day wore on, then shortly before last light there was a sudden energy up and down the line. Engines were fired-up, orders were barked, and slowly, inexorably, the convoy began to move. By now there were several civilian vehicles behind us. We bumped and squeaked our way through the checkpoint without being stopped and searched. There must have been some kind of deal struck by the convoy commander, because this place had a reputation for corruption and it was sometimes possible for a convoy to get through without too much delay if the asking price could be met. The UN rules dictated that bribes must be avoided. But then the rules were made by bureaucrats who didn't have to hang around for days on end at the roadside, I thought, so who could blame the soldiers for looking the other way when all it took was a few cartons of something attractive to fall off the back of a truck as a price for progress?

We were just a few kilometres past Rogatica when the Land Rover's engine began to cough and splutter. I pumped the accelerator thinking it was probably just a bit of dirty fuel, but the engine died. As hard as I tried, it refused to fire up again. It took an hour or so for us to realise that the old woman with the toothless grin must have part-filled the spare cans with water. But we were in luck because a pair of French armoured personnel carriers appeared behind us, and although the soldiers refused to give us a tow they allowed the major to travel with them into Sarajevo whilst I stayed with our stricken vehicle to prevent it being looted or stolen.

I noticed that the major had dropped the letter from Katarina's mother on the floor of the Land Rover, so I picked it up and hid it in my backpack to make sure it didn't get found at one of these checkpoints. Then I settled down to wait, drifting in and out of sleep as the day wore on.

Shortly before last light, Private Bagley and another driver appeared in a truck equipped with a tow-bar, and then we were driving slowly back towards the city with Bagley and myself in the warm cab and the second driver sat in the Land Rover behind.

"It's a cluster through the Sierra checkpoints," said Bagley. "Serbs are dicking around with another convoy, won't let it through."

"Inbound to Sarajevo?"

"Yes. It's taken them three days to get there from Goražde."

"We were stuck behind them for a while at Rogatica."

"Might take us some time to get back to the Residency. Be lucky to make it tonight."

The convoy ahead of us was moving slowly and fitfully into the city's outer suburbs when we caught up with it. We attached ourselves at the back, resigned to the idea of a long night. But the cab of the truck was warm and Bagley had brought along some stale sandwiches and a flask of lukewarm coffee, so we wouldn't be too uncomfortable.

"Lieutenant Harris has been asking about you."

"What did she say?"

"Nothing much. Just that she wants to jump your bones."

I replied with an expletive and Bagley chuckled. He continued to tease and I continued rising to his bait, but he didn't mean any harm by it because he was a good fellow after all.

The convoy was traveling on half-black, which meant dimmed headlights but not completely blacked-out. We didn't want to give the warring factions any thoughts that we might be the enemy. Ahead of us we could see the occasional tracer round flicking across the city.

The convoy stopped again, and exhaust fumes filled the night air because nobody wanted to turn their cab heaters off. Drivers were refilling cans from a fuel truck a little further along the convoy from our position. Once again, several civilian vehicles had tagged-on behind us, hoping maybe to ride with our convoy through the Sierras. I wondered vaguely if people were trying to get themselves across the lines of confrontation, or if they were simply smuggling contraband from one area of the city to another. Then I thought that smuggling themselves would be too risky because they'd probably be shot if caught.

So I concluded they must be in the business of transporting contraband because all they'd need to do then was bribe the checkpoint guards, and the most they'd risk would be having the goods confiscated. The checkpoint guards would be very unlikely to hurt them in front of all these soldiers from the United Nations Protection Force.

But suddenly I was proved wholly wrong in that, because a French armoured vehicle had been stopped just ahead of us at a Serb checkpoint and there was screaming and shouting and the cocking of weapons; and Frenchmen running up and down the convoy with their blue helmets bouncing on their heads and panic in their eyes.

Then there was a loud, sustained burst of automatic gunfire and the screams rising in guttural fear; then more gunfire and no more screams, but more shouting by the French and trucks revving their engines and pushing ahead, kicking up snow and ice with their wheels. We followed, with Bagley's jaw clenched tight and my rifle poking out of the window as we powered our way past the checkpoint.

We saw the French APC with its back door open and its internal white lights burning brightly, illuminating the scene outside. Two men and a woman lay dead on the ground, their bodies huddled in shapeless form, their blood splattered across the snow.

Serb soldiers were pulling apart suitcases stuffed with clothing and were aiming their guns at the French soldiers, who were running around screaming into their radios but not aiming their guns at the Serbs; and I could see that the French soldiers were hiding these people, and that the Serbs had found them and killed them and butchered them in cold blood at the side of the road; and the French soldiers could have done nothing unless they too had wanted to be shot, and where was the fucking the sense in all of this?

Bagley was shouting *bastards, bastards, bastards* as he urged the truck on and away. Then we were in the middle of the convoy with the fuel truck ahead of us, speeding along a stretch of clear road towards the city centre. My heart was racing because the screams of those poor people were ringing in my ears and because the guards at the checkpoint had seemed so fatalistically calm as they rummaged through the suitcases and held the French at bay.

Then the windscreen shattered into a thousand symmetrical pieces and our truck slewed to the left, pressing me hard against the door.

I looked towards Bagley, who was slumped over the steering wheel as if suddenly asleep. Then everything became the scene of an action film being played in slow-motion as the truck tipped hard over onto its side.

The remains of its windscreen came into the cab along with a deluge of slush and mud and ice that covered me and choked me. A huge brightness filled the crumbling cab as something exploded ahead of us. I knew this must be the fuel truck. I panicked with the thought that a river of fire would consume me and burn me, that I would die in pain and screaming agony.

I tried to struggle free, to get away; but the compacted snow and ice and glass had me trapped. The truck settled on its side. I heard the crackle of incoming high velocity and thought this must be an ambush. But how could this be an ambush? We were not at war with anyone, I wasn't sent to war, this wasn't our war.

But I was going to be killed in a war... *someone else's war*... and suddenly my ears were filled with a cotton-wool deafness as the percussive effects of a high explosive detonation blasted punched through my body. Then I was dizzy and loose and beyond control and beyond repair. Blackness closed in, darker than night, colder than death.

I floated, close to the edge.

My mind clawed its way back from the void. I opened my eyes and could see that Bagley was on top of me. I pushed at him and shouted at him, but I had no strength and could barely hear my own words. It felt like someone had hit me very hard in the ribs. My legs were trapped and my other arm was trapped. The smell of burning fuel was coarse and harsh, and the fear of being burned alive galvanised me into frantic action.

I pushed with my free arm against Bagley's shoulder. His head turned at an unnatural angle and his sightless eyes stared into mine. Bright, frothy blood oozed from his mouth and I realised he was dead.

I screamed a soundless scream, then twisted to try and disentangle my legs. Blinding, agonising pain stabbed upwards, taking my breath away. I knew I could not free myself. I wondered if this hunk of twisted steel and glass and snow and ice would be my coffin. Then I stopped moving and was beyond fear.

I passed in and out of a dreamless state.

The air was cold but Bagley's torso was warm, and in my waking moments I embraced him. I tasted his blood in my mouth. It was metallic and sweet. In the flickering light of the burning fuel I could see that the encroaching snow and ice was stained with more blood, but I did not know if this was Bagley's or mine.

The pain in my ribs was becoming acute. I noticed that I was coughing flecks of blood, and I thought my ribs must be snapped and sharp and sticking into my lungs. Or maybe this was Bagley's blood, but it was warm and I didn't think so.

I tried to keep my breathing shallow and regular but Bagley's body was unbearably heavy and by now it was becoming increasingly difficult to breathe at all. I wondered if maybe I'd suffocate under his weight and I thought that would be very strange because I had always considered him to be painfully thin.

Then there was bright white light, and muffled shouting; then shovels and hands and faces, and I was mouthing *I'm here, I'm here, I'm here…* and thinking, *please don't cut me with your shovels or kill me with your love…*

A face appeared that was vaguely familiar, and then Bagley's inert frame was being dragged clear. But even though his weight was no longer bearing down on me it was still difficult to catch a good strong breath.

Then more hands, gentler this time, holding me, feeling along the line of my side and down towards my legs; and then pain and a scream inside my head and a stab of morphine into my thigh and the slow spread of relieving warmth as the opiate took hold.

Professional hands, strong hands, capable hands. Clearing debris, straightening my limbs and straightening my back. Forcing some kind of board under my spine. I gritted my teeth and hung on. I tried to breathe slowly and I tried not to scream.

I could hear the sound of muffled foreign voices. I realised these must be Frenchmen, so I thought to myself *Vive la France!*

Then I knew that the familiar face was that of the English-speaking soldier from Mount Igman, and I wondered if he knew it was me, so I tried to speak. But the soldiers told me *Ne pas essayer de parler, monsieur.*

I coughed a little more blood that I now knew for sure to be mine. I tried to relax as they bound my legs and strapped me into their stretcher. They pushed a cannula into a vein and attached a drip. Then gently, incrementally, they hauled me from the wrecked truck.

Poor Bagley was laid on the ground like a discarded ragdoll. A French soldier was knelt by his side going through his pockets. I wondered if he was looting the body.

Then I was carried away past the burning fuel truck and loaded into an armoured vehicle. Someone stuck another shot of morphine into my thigh, and as the vehicle began to move I coughed more blood.

I closed my eyes and started to shiver, violently.

CHAPTER 10

"Your ribs are fine, but a small piece of shrapnel penetrated through the right side of your chest causing an internal bleed and the partial collapse of a lung."

The doctor was French, but his English was perfect.

"I am going to insert a one-way valve into your chest cavity," he continued. "It will help inflate your lung. It will hurt a little, and then you will feel some pressure."

The scalpel stabbed into my skin a few rib spaces down from my collarbone, somewhere above the nipple. My body squirmed and recoiled as the doctor sliced a hole an inch long. But my mind, dulled by the morphine, looked on with a curious air of detached interest; and then I understood that morphine doesn't so much take away the pain as help you care about it a little less.

Blood welled in the wound, and a medical orderly squeezed hard to staunch the flow. The doctor fussed with a sterile package then turned towards me with a device that resembled a large knitting needle. He pushed an end into the freshly opened hole, then leaned with almost all of his body weight to force the thing through the intercostal muscles and into my chest cavity.

My body gasped and rolled and the orderly helped to hold me down; and my detached mind told my trembling body to be still, and it was. Then the doctor withdrew the needle to leave something that looked rather like a condom hanging from the hole. He sutured the flesh together tight around the device. The orderly attached a hose that disappeared over the side of the table and my curious, conscious mind hoped they knew what they were doing.

The doctor unwound the crepe bandages wrapped around my legs. I glanced down and was relieved to see that both limbs were firmly attached to my torso.

"Now, this may also hurt a little." He lifted my right leg carefully but firmly with one hand behind my knee and the other grasping above my ankle. He articulated the leg through a normal range of motion and though I grimaced at the stiffness and the discomfort after so many hours having it immobilised, he seemed happy with what he found. "Now the other," he said, and this time I knew it was going to be a challenge.

I picked a tiny spot on the wall opposite, figuring it was probably a squashed fly or perhaps the body of a dead spider. I felt my leg being moved but there was no sharp pain, initially. Then it kicked-in, and then the morphine counted for nothing as the doctor tested for damage and watched for pain. In no way did I disappoint him. Vomit rose in my throat, and I struggled with my dignity.

"You were speeding through a checkpoint when you came under fire, correct?" The doctor was making small talk to try and divert my attention.

"That is not correct."

"No? It is what we heard."

"We were getting away from a bunch of Serbs who had shot an unarmed Muslim family dead at the back of a French armoured personnel carrier," I said through gritted teeth. "Then someone attacked us. I don't know who."

"Why didn't you try to stop them?" asked the doctor.

"Stop who?"

"The Serbs. Stop them from shooting the family."

"Why didn't your men try to stop them... oh, fuck..." The doctor was probing with his fingers along the side of my knee and had hit a sensitive spot.

"Here?"

"Yes, there..."

"A tragic situation," said the doctor.

"It's a bad injury?"

"The Serbs. Shooting people like that."

"Yes."

"Nothing much that anyone can do, really," he said.

Another probe, another shooting stab of pain.

"No, nothing much... Jesus..."

"You will need an operation. Not here."

The doctor motioned to the medical orderlies and they busied themselves debriding dead tissue around the grazes and cuts on my legs with scissors, then cleaning up and stitching without anaesthetic. By now I was almost past caring.

"If shrapnel passed through my chest, won't I need surgery?" I asked.

"Probably not," replied the doctor. "The lungs are very good at healing themselves. But if you become short of breath you must tell somebody straight away."

"If I can talk."

"Yes, if you can talk," he said.

"It's difficult to talk now."

"You are doing fine."

He finished up and then they wheeled me into a waiting area where a half-dozen other casualties from the convoy attack were sitting with various bandages dressing a variety of wounds. None of them were badly hurt, but I could see two body bags further along the corridor, one of which probably contained Bagley.

I asked for morphine, and after a short delay a medical orderly injected something into the cannula and the hit was almost instantaneous. I closed my eyes and slept.

The major visited shortly after first light and told me he was very sorry about Bagley, that he would write him up for a gallantry award and that I was very lucky to have survived the attack. And I thought, *a fat lot of good a medal will do him*, but then felt ashamed of myself because it would be very nice for his next of kin, whoever that may be, and agreed with the major that Bagley tried his best to evade the incoming fire and get us safely away from the ambush.

I asked who fired at us, and the major said it was the Serbs, of course. They'd opened fire because the convoy leader had panicked and sped towards the next checkpoint and we were mistaken by other Serbs for being a Bosnian convoy trying to breach the blockade. We were, he said, attacked as a legitimate target.

So I forgot my rank for a moment and asked him if that was an acceptable response from the Serbs, and the major had the grace to indulge my point of view because I had been hurt and was leaving this place anyway; and he told me *probably not*, so I felt that at least I'd scored a small victory in suggesting that anyone firing on a convoy carrying humanitarian relief to semi-starving people was probably in the wrong.

I asked about the rest of the Residency team, and the major told me everyone was on fine form and that the general was getting closer to having the warring factions talk about drafting some kind of agreement. I told him I was hoping to see Lieutenant Harris, but he said that wouldn't be possible because she'd been sent into Goražde to help the Observers there and probably wouldn't be back in Sarajevo for some weeks.

So I asked if he intended trying to find Katarina's father and his eyes glazed over a little, and I knew that the interview was done. So I thanked him for coming to see me, and he told me I'd receive a good report and wished me luck with getting my leg fixed. Then he left and I never saw him again.

The British based at Tuzla flew a helicopter into Sarajevo to lift us out. It remained at low level all the way up to Zagreb, where the US Navy were providing third line medical support to the UN. I knew the pilots had to be careful with a chest wound, but more importantly, one of the other wounded soldiers had a suspected fractured skull. Taking him to altitude could have killed him. So we risked being shot at with small arms fire by staying low, but the pilots were well practiced in the best route to use.

We touched down safely at the airport in Zagreb and were swept into the care of a comprehensive medical support system that saw most of the injured flown to their home countries that afternoon. But I was to remain with the Americans for several days because a decision had been made for my leg to be operated on here rather than back in England.

The injury had been confirmed as ligament damage, and the next week passed in a blur as I ground my way through the after-effects of surgery and came to terms with the idea of being off duty for some months. Then my bowels learned to re-engage, and everything became a stinking mess.

I tried to establish communications with the Residency, but it was impossible. Or if it was possible, I didn't have sufficient rank to access the limited communications system that connected the outside world to the centre of Sarajevo. All I could do was watch the news and speculate on its accuracy.

As the days passed, the visceral reality of that screwed-up place became no more than a fading memory. I found it very difficult to relate to life in either Bosnia-Herzegovina, or here in the pristine cleanliness and comfort of a hospital ward in Zagreb.

On occasion I awoke with images of Bagley's face pressed up hard against mine, his pale blue eyes staring into the void, his strangled breath fading away and the taste of his blood in my mouth.

Sometimes, I turned towards the wall and fought to hold back the tears.

A week later the sutures were removed from my grossly distended knee, the drain was taken from my lung, and the hole in my chest wall was sealed. A decision was taken to fly me home, and a friendly male nurse offered to push me around the city's streets with my leg bandaged tight in an open cast.

I found that Zagreb was alive and beautiful and cultured and elegant. Fast food outlets crammed up against shopping malls, leafless trees climbed high above snow-covered parks, and people strode to and fro dressed in brightly coloured clothing with pet dogs on leashes and happy children skipping along by their side.

We passed the United Nations headquarters, and I counted upwards of thirty white, spotless, brand-new limousines parked side-by-side with military precision, waiting to take various UN high-rankers back to their five-star hotels and three-course dinners, with wine and conversation in the lounge thereafter. The building, with its ornate columns, perfectly painted exterior and no doubt its lavish ballrooms inside, was a picture postcard.

The contrast with Sarajevo could not have been be more startling. I wondered how it was possible for any of these people to have an accurate understanding of how things were in the besieged capital of Bosnia-Herzegovina.

I slept my first dreamless sleep that night. In the morning I eat a small breakfast of pancakes drenched in maple syrup. Then a military ambulance took me to the international airport where a British Embassy official provided me with a temporary passport so I could clear Immigration. I was stretchered onto a Royal Air Force C130 that flew me and, unexpectedly, the dead body of Private Bagley, packed in dry ice, back to England.

CHAPTER 11

The Adjutant back at my parent unit told me that I was to be promoted sergeant with immediate effect and that everyone was very proud of me.

"But why?" I asked. "I didn't do anything."

"You acted very courageously."

"I did not, I was terrified."

"You were injured on operations. Your companion was killed."

I was confused, and certainly did not want to be thought of as a hero. "We got caught up in something by accident," I protested. "We shouldn't have even been there."

"You were part of a humanitarian aid convoy. You were ambushed, yet still tried to get through." The Adjutant was shuffling papers on his desk in an irritated fashion. "The Government made a statement. The country is doing its best in very difficult circumstances and sometimes our people get hurt, or tragically lose their lives. You did very well. Here are your sergeant's chevrons. You can wear them now."

"But..."

"Salute the officer, about turn, march out." The Regimental Sergeant Major's voice was as sharp as the creases in his uniform. I pocketed my new badges of rank, threw up a salute and complied with the rest of the RSM's directive as best I could without losing control of my wheelchair.

A few days later, I was ordered to see the Adjutant again. This time he shook my hand. Apart from my first meeting with the general in Bosnia, this was the first time an officer had afforded me this gesture since I'd enlisted.

He presented me with a small brown envelope that contained two bronze oak leaves, then handed me a cardboard certificate issued by Buckingham Palace. The certificate declared that I had been mentioned in dispatches for gallantry on operations. Having apparently been charged to record Her Majesty's high appreciation, the Secretary of State for Defence had signed it, personally.

I didn't have a chance to protest because this time the RSM wheeled me away, without delay.

Then it was Christmas, and I was sent on leave for a month whilst the surgery healed. I visited my parents, who seemed terribly excited that I'd received a gallantry award. I didn't even begin to explain, because news of the convoy ambush had been on the television and Private Bagley had been buried with full military honours. I'd thought about going to his funeral, but couldn't face up to the idea of having to describe for his family how he'd died. In any case, it was very nice that the Government seemed determined we should be seen as humanitarian heroes, at least for Bagley's family and I suppose mine too.

But I didn't feel like a hero and I didn't want to celebrate. In the stillness of the night I could still see Bagley's face, and sometimes I imagined I could hear the murdered family's terrified cries as the Serbs machine-gunned them to death.

The Army sent me in a hired car with my own driver to a military rehabilitation unit lodged in a country mansion to the south of London. I was carrying referral notes from the hospital that had assessed me on return to the UK. Security staff at the unit's main gate checked through their arrivals roster, but could find no mention of my name.

"You must be at the other place son, the one for non-commissioned ranks," they said. "This place is mainly for officers."

Calls were made, but somehow I seemed to be lost in the system. I sat in a small waiting room whilst the security staff tried and sort things out. I tried not to feel upset or angry, but had noticed since coming home that this wasn't always easy. A clock on the wall ticked loudly and I sat there marking time, wondering if I should think of leaving the Army. Or maybe I should have stayed on at school and achieved some qualifications, then joined-up as an officer instead of a grunt.

A tall and rather languid RAF squadron leader appeared, leafing through my medical notes. He was wearing his cap at a rakish angle and sported a thin moustache.

"Seems like we have a bit of a cock-up here, old chap," he said. "You should have been admitted to the other ranks rehab unit, but nobody told them and they're all chock-full right now." He glanced at my chevrons. "Hmm, sergeant eh? Says corporal here."

"Only promoted a few weeks ago, Sir."

"I see. Congratulations. Well, we have capacity here, and we do take Senior NCO's. Warrant Officers, usually. I called your unit and they say you were honoured for bravery in Bosnia. Would seem a bit heartless to turn you away."

So they admitted me, and now I was pleased that I'd been promoted and received an award.

I was allocated a bunk across the road from the main building, and spent a quiet evening as the sole occupant of a four-man room. The next morning, I hobbled across to a clinic located in what looked to be a converted stable, feeling quite out of place because this place was so beautiful. The main house, which was the Officers' Mess, looked like a small Elizabethan palace.

The clinic's staff were efficient and courteous, but not particularly kind. They wasted no time in cutting open my cast and prising it off.

I was shocked at the state of my leg. The scar was encrusted with dried blood, the knee was horribly swollen, and the skin of my leg was scaly and blue. I was directed towards another outbuilding and waited in an unheated corridor along with a half-dozen other patients all suffering from leg injuries. Then I was called into a small office where an RAF wing commander was poring over my medical notes.

"Tri-ligament rupture, classic vehicle accident injury, primary surgical repair," he said. "Plus a few lacerations… and it says here you had a partially collapsed lung plus a haemothorax. How is your chest?" He jumped up, not waiting for a response, indicating for me to remove my shirt. "Deep breaths." He listened through a stethoscope. "Seems OK. On the table."

I complied.

"This hurt?"

"Yes."

"Much?"

Gritted teeth. "Yes."

"Scale of one to ten?"

"Seven… no, eight… nine…" He was bending and twisting my injured leg without ceremony. I gripped the sides of the bench and broke into a sweat.

"OK, get down. Shirt on." He scribbled on my notes, then on a card. "Early knees. Flight Sergeant Williams. Main gym. See you again next Tuesday." He gave me the card, which was a weekly schedule for physiotherapy and rehabilitation. I left, and sought out Flight Sergeant Williams.

The flight sergeant was a stocky female physiotherapist who had a no-nonsense attitude and precious little sympathy. She wore a tracksuit and a scowl, and demanded total compliance with her schedule of exercises. The woman deployed devious manipulations and imposed cunning contortions that were in reality torture masquerading as therapy. I was in a class of fifteen, and we threw ourselves into her regime with varying degrees of enthusiasm.

"Woman is a sadistic bitch," said an Air Force flight engineer who'd broken his leg falling from a ladder whilst servicing the wing of a transport aircraft.

"She's just doing her job," I said.

"She's still a sadistic bitch."

"You'll get out of this what you put in."

"I'm putting in the least I can and will get out when they decide to medically discharge me," he said. "That way I'll get a decent war pension."

"Sounds like a good plan."

In the afternoon we split up into smaller groups for hydrotherapy, occupational therapy or one-on-one sessions with a dedicated physiotherapist. I discovered during the first one-on-one session that this variation of treatment would be the closest thing to genuine torture that existed in this place.

I found myself lying on a table that was encased by a wire cage. The physiotherapist attached my injured leg to springs that were clipped to the wire. These springs were in turn laden with small sandbags. The idea was to encourage my damaged knee to bend more than it was inclined to do. Within ten minutes I was drenched with sweat and hyperventilating because of the pain.

They took me out of the cage and iced my knee until it was numb. Then they put me back into the cage and spring-loaded me again until I was close to passing out.

"I told you, they're all sadistic bastards," said the flight engineer when we reconvened the larger class, and I thought by then that perhaps they were.

One night I had a visceral dream about Katarina's family in Žepa. I awoke covered in sweat and shaking like a leaf. In my dream I had seen them running away from their farmhouse across the snow-covered fields, being chased by Serb militia. The Serbs were shooting at them, closing them down, intent on murder. A group of French soldiers were standing by an armoured vehicle, leaning on their rifles and laughing. I had been shouting at them, imploring them to intervene, but they couldn't hear me because I was in the cab of an overturned truck and Bagley's body was on top of me.

I sat upright in my bed for an hour, calming myself down, trying hard not to wake anyone because by now the room had filled with patients and I was the junior rank. They wouldn't be pleased. Then I forced myself to lie down and close my eyes.

But it took forever to get back to sleep, and then all I could see was young Katarina's beautiful face staring with sightless eyes towards the cold grey sky as snowflakes settled on her pale, translucent skin.

The days and weeks rolled by, and slowly, inexorably, my withered leg began to gain strength and my shattered knee began to bend more effectively. I focused on the singular aim of becoming fit for duty, but the wing commander was brutally pragmatic about the prospects of such an eventuality.

"You're buggered," he declared, baldly. "Best you can hope for is a good functioning limb and a decent disability grading when the Army gets rid of you."

So I focused all my efforts on proving him wrong, and allocated myself incremental targets to demonstrate progress. Another five degrees of bend was a small battle won. Progression from crutches to sticks was a major watershed. The ability to walk a kilometre felt like an all-out victory even though increased pain and swelling was the penalty.

The weather improved and we moved from the gym to the gardens, which were formal and neat and clipped, and quite beautiful.

"We'll freeze our arses off out here," complained one of the patients. "Surely we'd be better off staying inside?"

But most of us much preferred to be outside. I breathed the clear English air and worked harder yet to show the wing commander how wrong he was. Some of the other patients saw that I was determined, and they stepped up their efforts too. I could see that I didn't have the worst injury here by any means. One of the men had lost a leg, and one of the women was missing an arm *and* a leg.

One day I struck up a conversation with Flight Sergeant Williams by asking why she had to be so disciplinarian.

"Because this is a military unit," she said. "And you people have to do as you're told, or else go away. If you don't conform to your schedule and put in enough effort, then you will not achieve a good result. And you'll be taking up a space that someone else could use. Someone with good motivation, someone who wants to get better."

"So you bully people to get them working?"

"To get them working harder," she said.

"You know they say mean things about you?"

"I don't care about that. They can say what they want."

"You're a good woman," I said.

She gave me an arch look. "And I'm a married one too. Just in case you were wondering."

"He's a very lucky man."

"Thank you. Now sod off to hydrotherapy."

I determined to throw my sticks away during our next class.

The evenings at this place were drab and boring. I played pool in the Warrant Officers' Mess, read books and watched TV. The news from Bosnia was consistently bad, and I tried to frame it out.

One day an Army warrant officer arrived and took up a recently vacated bed in my room. He introduced himself, and I could see from his red beret with its famous cap badge that he was from the Parachute Regiment. He was recovering from a cartilage operation and joined our class. It was immediately apparent that he had a maverick attitude towards authority and a well-developed dislike for malingerers.

"You're alright," he declared to me at the end of his first day. "You work your arse off. But the rest are just a bunch of lazy tossers."

"Oh, they're OK," I said.

"No they're not, they're a bunch of tossers."

The warrant officer had a car of his own, and although it was clearly painful for him to drive he insisted we make regular outings to towns that were within easy distance of the rehabilitation unit to drink beer and chat-up women. Life became more varied and more enjoyable, and within a couple of weeks, for the first time since arriving back in England, I began to feel that the Bosnia nightmare was drifting away from me.

I renewed my efforts and the wing commander seemed grudgingly impressed, so he accelerated me to the advanced knees category. Walking re-education gave way to the first stumbling steps of running. I could see that my leg muscles were gaining bulk and I could feel that they were gaining strength.

Then one day in mid-spring, with blue skies overhead and the gardens of the rehabilitation unit carpeted with bluebells and crocuses and daffodils and daisies, I was told to report to the security lodge. I towelled myself down, put on my uniform and followed the path around in front of the Officers' Mess towards the main gate.

Lieutenant Isabella Harris was there waiting for me, and in that moment my entire world stood still.

CHAPTER 12

"How did you know where to find me?"

We were walking through a quiet part of the gardens, down near the unit's brick-walled perimeter.

"It wasn't that hard," she said. "It was either the rehab unit down the road, back at your unit, or this place. It didn't take long."

"You look lovely," I said.

"I look tired."

It was true, she did look tired. Which was no surprise, because this was the first break she'd had from Sarajevo since I first met her there all those months ago.

"Why did you come?" I asked.

"Oh, you're such a child." She squeezed my arm tightly, and I laughed at my own naïvety.

"Then why didn't you write? Or call? Or get a message to me? I tried to reach you. You must know that."

"I wasn't sure how I felt. We heard you'd been killed. I was stuck in Goražde, so I didn't learn the truth for more than a week. Poor Bagley."

"Yes, poor Bagley."

"He was very brave."

"He was shot without warning," I said.

"It happens."

We stopped in a patch of warm sunlight and I drew her close. She hugged me, and her heart was beating like that of a small bird. I cupped her face in my hands and her eyes looked into mine. They were brimming with tears.

"How long do you have?" I asked, stroking her raven hair.

"Three weeks."

"You have to go back?"

"Yes."

"Then we don't have much time."

Her mouth was soft and open. We kissed, and I could taste the salt of her tears. I held her tight, pressing myself into her.

"Not here," she said.

"We had this conversation before." My breath was short.

"Later…"

She took me by the hand and led me back towards the main gate. I wanted her to stay, but she laughed and instead we made plans to meet again that evening in the town's only hotel. Then in full sight of the Officers' Mess and the security gate I saluted her and turned towards the gymnasium, resisting the urge to look back because I knew that people could be watching and it really was against the rules for an officer to have relations with an enlisted rank.

My Parachute Regiment friend with the car dropped me into town early in the evening without a question. Lieutenant Harris was waiting for me as promised at the hotel. She clutched at my arm, giggling nervously as we passed the young man at reception and climbed the stairs to a room that she'd booked for the next few nights. It was small but warm and comfortable, and had an *en suite* bathroom.

We undressed each other with trembling delight. Her skin was pale and soft. We stroked each other and kissed each other and touched each other with delicate uncertainty, then fell onto the bed and joined together with an energy born of sweet, shameless passion. The night had no end, her taste was sublime, and I knew that I was madly, deeply and impossibly in love with Isabella Harris.

We awoke late the next morning. I showered, then called for a taxi. Lieutenant Harris watched me from the bed with her grey eyes. She was wrapped in the duvet and was smiling mischievously.

"What will you tell them?"

"That I was detained and seduced by an Officer of the Crown," I said, pulling on my clothes and searching for my shoes. "That she wouldn't let me go, and I had to escape by climbing out of her bedroom window."

"They will be very impressed that you managed to do that with such a badly damaged knee." Her face was suddenly serious. "Does it hurt? It looks very angry."

"Not enough to stop me making love."

She laughed. "Not enough at all."

"You'll be here this evening?"

"Yes."

"Then I shall return as early as I can." I kissed her forehead. She reached up and grasped my wrist.

"This is real, isn't it?" she asked, and there was an enquiring urgency in her eyes.

"It is real," I said.

"It is, isn't it?"

"Yes." I kissed her again, headed for the door, then paused. "Why did you decide to come and see me?"

"Why do you think?"

"I asked first."

"Too many questions!" She threw a pillow at me. "Go to your rehab class. I'll tell you later."

The staff at the rehabilitation unit were surprisingly relaxed about my late arrival. I slotted-in at the back of the class and ground my way through the day's exercises, thinking all the time about Lieutenant Harris and feeling that this must all be some kind of delicious dream.

The warrant officer offered to drive me into town again when we'd finished, but I decided to order a taxi to keep things a little more discrete. Isabella was waiting for me in the hotel room and I held her immediately, wanting to make love. She kissed me hard on the lips, but then pushed me firmly towards the door.

"Food," she said. "I'm not a machine. And I just know you didn't have anything to eat before coming here, because you'd be in too much of a rush."

So we walked through the town and I wondered if any of the staff or patients from the rehabilitation unit would see us. But I didn't care if they did, because nothing was now more important to me that Isabella Harris.

We chose a sleepy restaurant and ate our food, gazing at each other shyly and talking quietly about Sarajevo.

"It's a mess," she said. "So many people being killed or injured."

"I try not to watch the news."

"You shouldn't. They almost always get it wrong."

"The reporters seem very much on the side of the Muslims."

"Yes, it's very unbalanced."

I tried to change the subject because I could see that it upset her, but she couldn't let it drop. I felt she needed to get away from there, and told her so.

"I have to go back. They need me," she said.

"Why?"

"They need people who can travel on all sides of the divide, speak to all the entities involved."

"They can find someone else."

"But there are so few of us. Serbo-Croat is hardly a popular language. And local interpreters can't cross the confrontation lines."

Our meal was done and the evening was wearing on. But she wanted to talk; and if she wanted to talk, then I would listen.

"I can speak the language because my family is from Yugoslavia," she continued. "My grandparents fled after the War, when Tito came to power."

"But your name is Harris. That isn't Yugoslavian."

"No, of course not," she said. "My grandparent's name was Stević. They were Royalist Serbs, Chetniks. So that's my mother's maiden name. She married an Englishman called Harris."

"Ah."

"Isabella isn't my real Christian name," she continued. "I was named after my grandmother. But having a Serb name could get me into trouble with the Muslims or Croats, so we had to change it when I first deployed with the UN."

"You're using a false name?"

"Yes. We had to get all my ID cards changed, even my passport."

"You're allowed to do that?"

"Of course."

"So what's your real name? Your real first name?"

"Miljana, but most people call me Milly. It's kind of inevitable I suppose."

I digested this for a moment. "It's pretty, but I prefer Isabella."

"So do I."

"Then you should keep it," I said.

"Maybe I shall."

We paid the bill, and walked slowly back to the hotel. The streets were dark, but it wasn't cold.

"You walk very well," said Lieutenant Isabella Miljana Harris. "How long before you return to duty?"

"The wing commander says a few more months."

"The wing commander? Who is he?"

"The man who said I was buggered. Evidently he's a god around here," I said.

"Well, he was wrong then. He needs to change his religion."

"To hell with religion."

"Amen to that."

We were getting close to the hotel. She stopped me and we embraced under a solitary streetlight.

We kissed, tenderly.

"Tell me why you came to see me."

"It was something you said. When we first met, when we walked along that ridge on the first day."

"I can't remember."

"You asked me why the war couldn't just end. Told me that everyone should just live in peace. It was so sweet, so innocent. In the middle of *that* place."

"I think I've lost my innocence."

"I said you would." Then she laughed out loud. "You've lost it in so many ways. Come on!"

We giggled our way past reception, up the stairs and into bed.

The days passed in a blur. We extended our hotel reservation. I worked at my routines and sweated on the rack, and every evening I returned to the hotel and talked long into the night with Isabella Harris. We paused now and then to make love, or to shower, or to eat and drink, or simply sit holding hands and savouring each passing minute as a precious moment stolen from time.

At the weekend we took a long drive in a car that she'd rented, out onto the South Downs with its green fields and rolling hills and quaint little villages, then away to the coast with its pebbled beaches and fishing fleets and fairgrounds and multicoloured sailing yachts.

"I love the yachts," said Isabella as we walked along the beach. "They're so bright and breezy and carefree."

"I used to sail," I said. "Started when I was a boy."

"I'd love to learn."

"I'll teach you."

"When your knee is better," she said.

"Yes."

"When your knee is much better."

"It will be, soon. I promise."

The following weekend I insisted that we take a train down towards the coast. Isabella was intrigued but excited in a sweet kind of way, so different from the tired and stressed woman who'd arrived back home from Bosnia.

"What are we going?" she asked.

"You'll see."

The train pulled into a country station and we disembarked with our small overnight bags. Isabella was almost beside herself with excitement.

"It's a mystery journey!" she exclaimed, holding hard on my arm and almost skipping along the platform.

"Yes, it is," I said. "Who knows where it will end?"

We followed a narrow path away from the station and down towards a river, then along a muddy lane and through a yard that was strewn with junk and the rotting remains of abandoned boats. We slipped around the edge of a fence and climbed a rickety staircase onto the terrace of an imposing public house, then made our way to the end of a jetty, and down more stairs onto a narrow floating pontoon with yachts moored to left and right.

"What are we doing?" asked Isabella.

"You'll see. Quick, grab this." I reached down into the water and pulled up a length of slippery rope. She took it from me, holding it as if it was some kind of disgusting thing, which it was. "Now, pull," I said.

So she pulled, and the line rose from the water, clear across a twenty-foot gap towards a midstream pontoon. A small floating platform came across, and it arrived on our side with a thump. Then we stepped onto the platform, giggling like children and holding onto each other because it was horribly unstable. I told her to drop the line, which she did, and a counterweight pulled us slowly but surely to the midstream pontoon where we stepped off without losing our footing even though it was slippery and wet.

"There she is," I said, pointing towards a small sailing yacht. "Ours for a day."

Isabella looked at the yacht, looked at me, and then with a squeal of delight ran towards it and slipped, but caught herself on the boat's gunwhale and didn't fall into the water. I helped her to her feet, and she was laughing and smiling and in a moment we were onboard, packing away our bags and laughing some more. I explained to her how everything worked and told her that we'd drift down with the ebb tide to a nice marina at the mouth of the river and stay there overnight.

We hanked-on a number two genoa and prepared the main on its halyard, then let go the lines and drifted out into the flow of the tide, turning full-circle as I struggled with the hoist. The sail filled and I sheeted-in, then Isabella hoisted the genoa and we sheeted that in too.

A gentle breeze pushed us out into the fairway and the river was calm, so we settled together on the helm and glided down the river with its clustering trees and countless yachts moored to midstream pontoons or mud-driven piles; and Isabella's hair played around her face as the swans and the geese paddled along behind us until they tired in our wake and dropped far astern.

"Let's not go to the marina," said Isabella. "Let's stay on the river. It's so beautiful out here."

"But we don't have anything to eat," I said. "Or drink."

"You have me..."

She turned towards me and kissed me full on the mouth. I lost control of the helm and we rounded-up, all taken aback and wallowing badly. Then she was on top of me and the boom was thrashing to and fro over her head. I tried to push her off but she wouldn't let go. The yacht drifted into the riverbank and her bilge-keels stuck in the mud, and with our sails flapping wildly we made the sweetest of love on a fast-falling tide with no hope of going anywhere until the evening flood.

I returned to the rehabilitation unit and asked the wing commander if I could take some leave.

"Fed up with the place already?" he asked, but not in a nasty kind of way.

"I feel like I've reached a plateau, Sir," I replied. "Might be good to give things a rest."

"Learning the rehab language, eh?" he said. "Good man. Everyone reaches a plateau in this game at some point. OK, take a couple of weeks. Be careful with that knee."

I reassured him that I'd be very cautious and returned to the hotel that evening bursting with the news and filled with happiness that I could now devote all my time and energy to Isabella Harris.

We checked out the next morning and drove across the top of the day to her mother's house on the far side of the country. I knew by now that her father had died when she was a small child, and that her mother never remarried.

"You'll like my mother," she said. "But don't be surprised if she asks you a million questions. She's very smart, and has been trying to marry me off for years."

"Then maybe we should indulge her."

"Is that a proposal?"

"Do you want it to be a proposal?" I asked.

"Only if you want."

"That's what I want."

"Then I'll think about it."

"Don't think for too long," I said.

"Why not?"

"We could get married before you go back to Bosnia if we hurry."

"It's against Queens Regulations," she says.

"What is?"

"An officer marrying an enlisted rank."

"The to hell with Queen's Regulations," I said.

She laughed. "OK. I'll think about it. But that wasn't exactly a romantic proposal."

She had a point.

Isabella's mother was small, dark-haired, and had the same slate-grey eyes as her daughter. She shook my hand, coolly but firmly.

"You're the first boyfriend that Miljana has ever brought home," she said. "What makes you so special?" It seemed strange to hear Bella being called by her real name.

She sat me down at the kitchen table and fired off a few dozen questions, all the while avoiding any mention of Bosnia, yet teasing out of me all the salient facts that a mother might be interested to hear about her young daughter's suitor. I liked her. She was indeed very smart, and not at all put-off when she learned that I was just a sergeant.

"Miljana's grandfather was a sergeant during the war," she said while Bella was unpacking her bag. "We were all very proud of him."

That evening Isabella Miljana Harris and I took a slow walk across the fields down to a small river that was flowing past a local church.

"I used to come down here and play when I was a child," she said. "My father is buried in the churchyard. I thought I could talk to him, so I'd tell him all about the rotten kids at school. I thought he could speak to me too, so I used to hear all the words I wanted to hear. He was the perfect Dad."

"Do you want to go and say hello now?" I asked.

"No. I realised eventually that he really was dead, and wasn't coming back. So I stopped going."

"That sounds so sad."

"I guess he must have loved me. That's good enough."

We turned away from the church and followed the river downstream a little, then cut up back across the fields towards the house. The sun was dipping towards the horizon and the air was becoming chill. I pulled Isabella close and she leaned against me. I wanted to stop and kiss her, but she suddenly pulled away and started running.

"Come on," she said. "Dinner must be nearly ready!"

I began to run after her, but my knee complained so I walked again. Isabella stopped and let me catch up.

"I'm so sorry," she said, and there was real concern in her voice. "I forgot about your knee."

"It's OK," I said. "Next time we visit I'll run all the way to the river and back again."

"Yes, you will," she said. "You will be fit and strong and all repaired, and you'll be able to go down on your bended knee and propose in a manner befitting a lady like me."

Yes, I thought. That's exactly what I'll do.

The days here were bright and full of laughter and stories about the family and stories about Isabella growing up. I got along with her mother famously. The longer we stayed the more I was certain that somehow Isabella and I would make this situation work out, that we were meant for each other, and to hell with the Army.

I suggested that we continue driving north. Isabella pulled out a tent and some sleeping bags from the attic. We swept out the cobwebs and dead spiders and tested everything in the garden, then we found some pots and pans and a cooker that worked. We said goodbye to her mother, who gave me a strong, searching look and a solid hug before kissing my cheek and telling me to take good care of her girl.

Isabella insisted on driving because she was worried about my knee, and as we reversed away from the house her mother was waving from the garden and I waved back. Then we were on the road and heading away, and the air was warm and the road ahead clear.

CHAPTER 13

The rain beat down on the roof of the tent, sending rivulets of water running down its sides. It was cold outside. But in here, in the arms of Isabella Harris, everything was cosy and comfortable and safe and warm. It had been raining all night in that persistent, Scottish kind of way. The wind was buffeting around the hills as a new front came galloping through from the west.

Isabella stirred.

"Are you awake?" I asked.

She mumbled something and stretched, then settled and hooked a leg across my stomach, naked and deliciously soft. I stroked her wonderfully smooth skin and luxuriated in the sensation of feeling her body pressed against my side. I traced the palm of my hand across the contours of her athletic backside, then drifted to sleep, wrapped in her warmth.

We packed away the tent once the front had passed and the air was fresh and clear. The clouds had scudded away to the east and the distant sea was breaking on the shore. The heather was purple and bright, and I knew that soon the midges would rise and that if we stayed too long we would be driven crazy as they began to bite.

"Let's drive down to the coast and follow the road to the end of the peninsular," I said. "There must be a great view from out there."

So we loaded up the car and followed the narrow, winding road until it became a narrow, winding track. It climbed inland across the moors and past the lakes, ever westwards, towards the ocean.

"How do you say the name of this place again?" asked Isabella.

"Ardnamurchan," I said. "There's a lighthouse at the end of the track. It's the most western point of the mainland."

"How do you know that?"

"I just know."

"You're very clever."

"I'm a man of the world."

It had been a lovely journey to this remote and windswept place, but time was beginning to press and we needed to be heading south again very soon. It was a week since we'd said goodbye to Isabella's mother, and in a few days Lieutenant Harris would have to begin her journey back to Bosnia.

I shuddered at the thought of the place. But then had to check myself, because Bella had told me something of its history, and the blood of those people ran in her veins. Not everything was bad. It was just the politics that was bad… and the religion… and the people… or some of them, at least.

I checked myself again. I needed to concentrate on the here and now, on the mission of the day. Because I did have a mission, a reason for bringing her here.

Railed steps descended from the lighthouse towards the edge of the cliff. The wind was blowing strongly around the headland. The air was salt-laden and heavy. Breakers were crashing onto the rocks below, sending spray high into the air that caught the sun and cast fragmented rainbows across the sky.

"This is fantastic!" shouted Isabella, running ahead and down the steps. "Look at all the waves, look at the seagulls… come on slowcoach, try and keep up!"

I tried to run after her but quickly realised that wouldn't work. So I hobbled along, being careful not to stumble or fall because I didn't want to return to the rehabilitation unit in a worse condition than when I left.

When I reached her, Bella was looking down towards the sea with her hair blowing all over the place and her knuckles white on the rail. She turned towards me and threw her arms around my neck and we kissed; and her nose was cold and her eyes were wide and I fell inside them and drowned. I pushed her away and caught my breath, then reached into my pocket and knelt as best I could. I held out the ring and asked her if, in all sincerity and in the face of all difficulty, she would consider marrying me.

Isabella Harris stepped back and covered her mouth with her hands and looked at me with those big grey eyes. Then she nodded her head and I could see that her eyes were not sad, but they did have tears; and the tears were not the tears of sorrow, but of joy. I struggled to my feet and we embraced. I placed the ring on her finger and it was a perfect fit. The wind played around us as the sea crashed onto the rocks below; and a bright, solid rainbow arced suddenly across the clear blue sky.

We journeyed south and laughed and joked and hugged and stopped three more times to sleep in our tent with its musty smell of damp sleeping bags and unwashed clothes. But as we got closer to the Air Force base from where Isabella would return to Sarajevo she became increasingly quiet and withdrawn.

At first I thought it was something I'd said or something I'd done, but she assured me it wasn't and that I didn't need to worry because I was a very sweet boy and she wouldn't have agreed to marry me if I wasn't. But she began to chew at her nails and started smoking again. As we checked into a hotel for one last night together before she left, it felt like she was drifting away from me.

"Do you really have to go?" I asked. "You've done enough over there, Bella, really you have."

"I'll finish when it's over," she responded sharply. "There's still a lot to be done."

"We'll have to tell them we're engaged though," I said. "Won't that be a problem?"

"We don't have to tell anyone. I forbid you to tell anyone."

I thought she was joking, but she wasn't.

She took off the ring and slipped it in her purse. "See, there," she said. "Now only you and me know. We can sort all that out when I come back."

I wanted to argue the point, tell her it was ridiculous. But I wasn't brave enough. I didn't want to upset her. I could see she was stressed. We could get married later on. She must do what she must.

I lay awake for most of that night, listening to her breathing and watching her face. She was so beautiful. Her face was serene. But occasionally she twitched and then scowled and I thought she was about to wake. But then she settled and fell once more into a deeper level of unconsciousness. And I wanted to kiss her and hold her, but she did need to rest.

After breakfast she put on her uniform and packed her Army bag ready for her flight. I drove her to the Air Force base and my knee handled the clutch just fine. She didn't want me to come onto the base with her, so we parked out of sight from the gate. She pecked me on the cheek and was gone very quickly and I felt terribly hollow.

I drove to Heathrow and dropped off the rental car, then paid a ridiculous amount of money for a taxi ride to the rehab unit and learned that my Parachute Regiment friend had been discharged, but that the malingering flight engineer was still there.

CHAPTER 14

I recommenced my daily rounds of physiotherapy and hydrotherapy and occupational therapy and solo sessions on the torture rack. The days merged into weeks and I became increasingly miserable because my heart was in a different place. But I was determined to become fit again.

I took a fall one day trying to run through the woods to the top of a hill outside the grounds of the mansion. My knee swelled horribly and its range of movement regressed to less than ninety degrees. I became more depressed, and drank in the evenings and watched the television news for any mention of Sarajevo. I was worried sick about Isabella because I heard nothing from her, and had no way to get in touch apart from sending letters. I was devastated that she never replied.

The knee didn't respond well to treatment, so the wing commander decided to send me back to the military hospital where the doctors manipulated it under a general anaesthetic. I awoke from the procedure in desperate pain. They had forced the joint to bend through its full range of movement then strapped my heel to my backside using thick bandages.

The pain was agonising, like a sharp knife slicing through my thigh from knee to groin. I writhed and moaned and sweated as if trapped in a sauna. The morphine didn't help. The nurses were sympathetic but unyielding. Every hour, a physiotherapist came to the ward, released the bandages, straightened my leg, and then forced it to bend again as far as he was able before strapping it into position and rolling me onto my side. I shivered and shook and tried not to vomit.

But by the end of twenty-four hours everything was back to less than ninety degrees, and by the end of the second day I had even less flexion than when I'd arrived here. I was totally exhausted at the lack of sleep and relentless pain.

The ward sister decided that enough was enough. She released the bandages, straightened my leg, and I fell into a fathomless sleep that prevailed through the remains of the day.

On my return to the rehabilitation unit there was much debate between the various departments about how best to proceed. They decided to regress me to the early knees class. I trod the same trail, endured the same programme of discomfort and pain, and in time I got back to the same point of rehabilitation I'd reached before my fall in the woods.

"You can't outrun the biology," said the wing commander as he moved me into the pre-release class. "Stick with your schedule and you'll be fine."

The rhododendron bushes were beginning to bloom and spring had turned towards the early promise of summer when I took the Army's battle fitness test. I pounded the circuit, trying to outstrip other patients who were carrying less serious injuries than mine. I managed to come home in the middle of the pack and knew that I was done with this place. The wing commander agreed, and I was directed to report back to my parent regiment for light duties.

A military bus delivered me to the local railway station a few days later. On the train I watched the lush green fields of England roll by as I gathered my thoughts and structured my arguments. Because by now I knew there was only one place I wished to be.

The Adjutant looked at me as if I had descended from the moon.

"You want to go where?"

"Back to Sarajevo, Sir."

"You're restricted to light duties, Sergeant. Here, at the depot."

"That's not what I want, Sir."

"Well, that's what you've got."

Interview over, case dismissed.

I returned to my room in the Sergeant's Mess and reviewed my options.

Leave the Army.

Go absent from the Army and make my way to Bosnia.

Or wait for Lieutenant Harris to finish her tour of duty in Sarajevo and then reconnect when she got home.

The last of these was the sensible course of action. Only I didn't know when she'd be back, and I ached for her, yearned for her. It was a non-starter. There had to be some other way.

The answer, when it came, was wholly unexpected. I was called to the Adjutant's office. He was sat there, clearly upset. He had a piece of paper in front of him, a signal from some superior Command within the Army.

I was on orders to report to the United Nations Protection Force in Bosnia-Herzegovina, with immediate effect. I had been reassigned to the UN Observers.

CHAPTER 15

The Royal Air Force C130 transport aircraft went into a steep dive, descending several thousand feet at an impossible angle to minimise the risk of being hit by small arms fire on its final approach to Sarajevo. We had been briefed to anticipate this, to sit on our flak jackets with their steel-plate inserts and hope that we didn't receive a penetrating high velocity welcome through our backsides.

The aircraft fired off streaming clusters of chaff as we descended, tinfoil distraction devices that would hopefully fool any heat-seeking missiles that may have been streaking towards us. Spent chaff rained down upon the frontline suburb of Ilidža, damaging roofs and generally annoying the residents, who in turn fired off their weapons at us in anger. To my mind, this did not seem like a win-win situation.

The aircraft straightened out at the last safe moment and landed with an almighty thump on the rough tarmac, engines feathering and brakes locking. We shuddered to a halt and turned towards the battered terminal building as the stern ramp went down. I could see an Ilyushin heavy transport aircraft down on its nose at the end of the runway, victim of an accidental overshoot and now wholly unmovable. It looked like a victim of the war fighting, which it was not.

The warrant officer was waiting for me as I emerged from the terminal building. He looked tired and drawn, but smiled when he saw me and shook my hand. He was driving the same Land Rover that had broken down on the way back from Žepa. I could see that it must have been badly damaged when the truck turned over. But it had been repaired well enough, and soon we were headed into the city centre.

The weather was warm and dust was rising from the road. Even though the year was moving towards summer, the same dirt-filled haze hung in the air and the surrounding hills had lost none of their menace. I found myself trembling momentarily, caught by bad memories and a transient, irrational fear. But then the feeling was gone.

"How is your leg?" asked the warrant officer.

I lied to him that everything was fine, and asked how things had been progressing with the Observer mission.

"We have a different general, and a new major," he said. "Many things have changed since you were last here. You'll see."

"Changed for the better?"

"They've just... changed."

"And Lieutenant Harris. She's still here?"

"No, she's gone."

My heart dropped towards the floor of the vehicle.

"Gone where?"

"To Zagreb... but she'll be back in a few days. She did recommend you. Was quite insistent, actually."

I could see that the warrant officer had a humorous glint in his eye. I wondered how much he knew, and I wondered how much he could guess.

I found that I'd been allocated the same bunk in the same cabin that I'd previously occupied. I dropped off my pack and headed for the office.

"Don't you knock, Sergeant?" asked the new major.

I could immediately tell by his tone that things had indeed changed. I apologised, and wondered if I should be saluting. The major rubbed his eyes in a manically intense kind of way, turned back to his desk and continued scribbling his notes. I felt he must have been stressed and exhausted, so I forgave him. But that was the last time he ever spoke to me.

The warrant officer told me that my duties would largely involve driving reconnaissance missions around the city, that the situation appeared to be deteriorating, and that it was very likely the Muslims and the Serbs would be moving back to a condition of war very soon. I asked why the ceasefire should be breaking down and which side was the aggressor, but a hard stare from the major ended that conversation in its tracks. So I left the office and took a tour of the Residency to remind myself of its layout.

Little seemed to have changed. The Danes were still responsible for its security, and I could see that more sandbags had been laid down and the blast walls had been further fortified. A Danish soldier informed me that in the event of a direct attack on the compound, everyone would be moved into a road tunnel located behind an adjoining building. He said that the tunnel's mid-section had been blocked by the Bosnian Army because they had a tank hiding at the far end that emerged occasionally to fire a few rounds towards the Serb lines in the hope of provoking a response.

I wandered into the canteen to see if we still had the same head waiter and chef, but they've been replaced. An irate cleaner pointed to a meal schedule pinned to the wall and told me that the canteen was off limits outside these hours and that I needed to get out because he had to disinfect the place and deal with all the damned flies that were contaminating the food. He flicked at me with a filthy, contaminated mop and said didn't I think it was damned hot in here, and didn't I know there might not be a full meal that evening because the latest convoy had been held up for three days by the damned Serbs, and that even if it got through didn't I know that all the damned fresh food would be rotten?

I retreated to my cabin and spent the rest of the day dozing fitfully. A small electric fan stirred the limpid air and the springs of my bunk squeaked every time I shifted position.

Late that evening, the warrant officer joined me and said that we'd be leaving early to see if we could loosen things up for the convoy stuck at Sierra One. I went down to check the Land Rover. The air was much cooler but not cold, and in the distance I could hear intermittent gunfire.

So I thought that the only big difference in this place since I'd left was the fact that nobody was freezing to death.

We set out the next morning soon after first light and only reached the Serb checkpoint at Sierra One after being held-up by the French, who appeared to have renewed their concern about peacekeepers traveling around in soft skinned vehicles. I tried deploying the bulletproof fabric argument, but the soldiers pointed out several bullet holes in the canvas that I'd not noticed and my credibility was blown. The warrant officer raised our headquarters on his radio, and after an hour of delay the French received the required permissions through their own chain of command and lifted their barrier with a dismissive *allez, vite!* We arrived at Sierra One as the Serb officers were taking breakfast, and were made to wait by our vehicle until they were done.

Fifty or more dust-covered UN trucks were parked on the far side of the checkpoint barrier. Bored soldiers and civilian drivers lounged around, unshaven, unwashed and wholly resigned to the tedium of their predicament. They stood in groups chatting, or sat on boxes cooking up breakfast on hexamine stoves. A few were sat in the cabs of their vehicles, reading or dozing. Further along the line I could see another group playing soccer with a partially inflated ball whilst children watched from the side of the road.

Serb guards ambled up and down the line of vehicles with rifles slung easily over their shoulders, cigarettes hanging from their mouths. A few of them were talking with truck drivers, asking for smokes or drinking beer from crumpled tin cans. Some of the vehicles had improvised canopies slung from their roofs, and the whole scene was lit by yellow sunlight that warmed the morning air. The barrier remained firmly down, its chain padlocked shut.

This is the story of the United Nations Protection Force, I thought to myself. Well-meaning men and women delivering vital supplies through these chokepoints; uncaring soldiers blocking their way; politicians and generals juggling with the fortunes of nations as the civil population suffered or died.

Looking at all these trucks and all these men, sent here by the international community to deliver simple humanitarian relief, it occurred to me that goodwill alone would never be enough to bring a lasting peace to this place.

A hotel-like building located directly alongside the barrier but set back from the road was the Serb headquarters for Sierra One. We could see soldiers or police looking out occasionally through its grimy windows, sometimes at us, sometimes at the convoy. We had been told to wait.

So we waited, and the warrant officer told me that they would get around to speaking with us eventually because they were under orders from the Serb Presidency to negotiate the release of the convoy. I wondered how the warrant officer knew this, but I supposed he'd been told by the major or perhaps even by the general himself. Then it occurred to me that I hadn't even seen the new general yet. I wondered if he was as good as the last one, or worse; or perhaps just the same. Or if it even mattered.

The sun was climbing towards the middle of the sky when the door to the Serb headquarters finally opened. A woman wearing a purple and black combat uniform walked down the steps, picking at her teeth, not in a hurry. She wandered slowly across the parking area, waving ineffectually at a small cloud of flies gathering around her head, then stopped just a few feet away from us. She canted her head to one side, and smiled at us, slyly.

"You are from the Residency?"

She was wearing an officer's peaked hat, perched at an awkward angle on top of her fluffed, peroxide blond hair. Her uniform was shapeless but pinched tight at the waist by a belt from which there hung an automatic pistol encased in a thick leather holster. Hairs sprung from the bridge of her nose and, alarmingly, from her upper lip and chin. Put simply, she had a beard.

"Yes, ma'am," said the warrant officer.

"You want to talk about the trucks?" she asked.

"We do."

"So do I." She stroked her bearded chin, then looked at me seductively and smiled again. Her teeth had been bleached white, but were stained tobacco-brown on the right side of her mouth. "Who is the little boy?"

"My driver."

She reached forward and unfastened the top button of my combat jacket. I recoiled, but she persisted.

"Maybe he has a little gift for me?"

The unmistakable smell of *Slivovica* was on her breath. The warrant officer reached in through the Land Rover's window and produced a carton of cigarettes.

"This good?" he asked.

The bearded woman took the carton and stuffed it inside her uniform, then reached back to me and stroked my face. "Perhaps your young friend would like to come inside for breakfast?"

I thought, *oh my god, is this creature offering me sex?* But the warrant officer asked her about the convoy's current status and then her smile was gone and she was all business-like and iceberg-cold.

She harangued us for five minutes without pause, telling us how the UN was smuggling contraband to the Muslims, accusing us of conspiring with the Bosnian Government and encouraging the USA to use their aircraft against her people, screaming that very soon now the goodwill of the Bosnian Serb Army would be exhausted and then no convoys at all will be allowed to pass through. Then she strutted back to the hotel and slammed the door behind her.

The warrant officer took all this without flinching or responding. When she'd gone, he got on the radio then told me that we may as well relax because a high-ranking deputation was on its way from the United Nations headquarters in the nearby town of Kiseljak.

The deputation, when it arrived late that afternoon, was led by the new general. His close protection team swept-in first, all sunglasses, flak jackets, machine-guns and energy.

The Serb guards responded by unslinging their rifles and concentrating around the road barrier, but they didn't seem particularly anxious. It seemed they were quite used to this kind of scene.

Then the general's vehicle arrived and he stepped out with his personal protection officer and Lieutenant Harris. They walked directly up to the warrant officer. I tried to catch Isabella's eye, but she studiously ignored me. She seemed tense and exhausted, and I was shocked by her appearance. I wanted to say something to her, reach out to her, but I realised she was wholly focused on what needed to be done here and that I was irrelevant to her task.

The warrant officer described what had happened thus far. The general listened attentively, asked a few considered questions, then told the lieutenant to have the Serb checkpoint commander come and speak with him. Isabella walked across to the hotel entrance and disappeared inside.

We waited for a full twenty minutes before she emerged with the bearded lady and two other Serb officers. The Serbs looked angry and grim. Lieutenant Harris looked drawn and pale, and I could see her hands clenching and unclenching. I was close enough to see that her fingernails were chewed and broken and I cared enough to realise that she was close to the edge.

The exchange between the general and the Serb officers was terse. The checkpoint guards began to look agitated, handling their weapons nervously and staring at their feet. The general's bodyguard team remained in position, focused and professional. They were widely dispersed, and I could see they had taken up mutually supportive arcs of fire. I stepped back towards the Land Rover thinking that if anything kicked-off I could use it as cover and be of some use with my pistol, though I didn't really have the training for that.

The Serb officers walked back to the hotel to confer with their Presidency. They returned a few minutes later. The bearded woman screamed at the general for a full two minutes without seeming to take a breath, then confirmed that the convoy would be allowed through.

The warrant officer walked smartly across to brief the convoy commander, a young British officer who by now had marshalled all his drivers back into their cabs. The officer ran along the line of trucks shouting instructions, and the drivers began firing-up their engines. Clouds of exhaust fumes rose towards the clear blue sky and children appeared at the side of the road asking one more time for candy as the checkpoint barrier lifted.

The general and his close protection team mounted into their vehicles, but I could see that one of the Serb soldiers had caught Lieutenant Harris by her arm, pulling her off to one side. I stepped towards them; then ran towards them because I could see that the bearded woman was unbuckling her leather holster.

The general's convoy was moving and the trucks were beginning to roll. Noise and exhaust fumes filled the air. The Serb soldier was twisting Isabella's arm, forcing her towards the ground. I reached them and my gun was out and jammed into his face; then the warrant officer was at my side with his gun out too, pointed at the bearded creature, and we had Isabella between us, dragging her away. The other Serb guards were reacting, cocking their weapons and closing us down. Then Isabella twisted herself away, ran straight back to the bearded woman and punched her in the face.

In that moment I thought we are all about to die.

But the bearded woman barked an instruction to the guards and they held off, lowering their weapons. The warrant officer and I grabbed Isabella again and pulled her towards the Land Rover. The bearded woman picked herself up, straightened her uniform and crammed her ridiculous hat back on top of her head. Then she smiled at us like a wolf, blood oozing from the corner of her mouth, and dismissed us with a wave of her hand.

We loaded the lieutenant into the back seat of the Land Rover and I jumped in with her. The warrant officer gunned the engine and we joined with the convoy. Isabella buried her head into my chest and hugged me tight. I kissed her dust-filled hair and it bore the smell of her sweat, mingled with that familiar hint of lavender.

CHAPTER 16

"She was accusing me of being a traitor," said Isabella. She was sitting on my bunk with a mug of lukewarm tea clasped in her hands. A half-smoked cigarette trembled between her nicotine-stained fingers. "She said they know my family history, know that I have Serbian blood. Said my grandfather was a deserter, and that I'm a Muslim spy."

"So we have the general get you out of here, send you home," I said.

She laughed, a nervous, anxious laugh. "That will never happen."

"Why not? That woman threatened your life. You're an officer in the British Army, Bella. We have a duty of care…"

"We have a duty *not* to care." She took a long draw on her cigarette, and closed her bloodshot eyes. "Our duty is to the mission."

"But surely this means you can't deal with the Serbs anymore? It's too dangerous!"

She opened her eyes and laughed again. "It's the first time the Serbs have threatened me directly," she said. "But the Bosnians have been doing that for months and nothing has happened."

"The Bosnians too?"

"They know I have a Serbian ancestry. They even know my real name."

"You have to get out of here," I said. "Something bad will happen, I know it will. These people are monsters. They don't care who they hurt. I've seen them kill people, innocent people."

"You've seen nothing," she said, dousing her cigarette in the remains of her tea. "But we have to carry on, I have to carry on. There's too much at stake. So many people's lives hang in the balance…"

And then she was crying, so I pulled her close and we sat there until the warrant officer came in and told us that he'd spoken with the general and that the lieutenant would be kept away from the dark side for a while, that he'd find someone else to liaise with the Serbs.

Then she left, and the warrant officer didn't ask why I was hugging her. So I offered him a beer, which he accepted, and we chatted about nothing in particular until the night drew in and it was time to sleep.

True to his word, the general did keep the lieutenant away from the Serb side over the coming weeks. She busied herself around the Residency and with the Muslims, though I couldn't help feeling she must be equally at risk from these people if they'd identified her family origins and had already threatened her life. It was difficult to have quiet or intimate moments together in the claustrophobia of this place, so we danced around each other with a charade of formality camouflaging the truth of our relationship.

One day I happened upon the letter that Adnan's mother had given me in Žepa. In the confusion of everything and what with being back in England for so many months, I had completely forgotten my promise. Now there it was, hidden in a compartment of my backpack, crumpled and frayed around the edges but otherwise undamaged.

I showed it to Isabella and told her about Adnan and his beautiful young sister and his splendid grandparents, and his mother with the hairy arms. Isabella took the letter and promised to try and track down Adnan's father, or at least find out where he might be. I was pleased by this, because it would give her something to take her mind away from what she called 'failing to do her duty' in being restricted to the Muslim side of the confrontation line. I then forgot for a while about the letter and my promise to Adnan's mother.

But I could not forget his young sister's amazing green eyes or the beauty of her smile.

In the city we were experiencing an increased level of sniper fire, interspersed with the occasional mortar or artillery attack. Tension was rising and the days were becoming longer and more dangerous as the snipers concentrated their firepower on the civil population.

I visited the Serb frontlines on one of our reconnaissance missions, and learned that the snipers ran sweepstakes on their targets. That day, the targets of choice were children. Yesterday, it had been anyone wearing the colour yellow. Tomorrow it might be anyone seen riding a bicycle.

I was appalled by the brutality of all this, but to the soldiers it seemed to be one big joke, and they laughed and played cards and drank *Slivovica* between shoots. The officers helped to spot their targets, and I was told that the snipers would laugh with excitement at the sheer pleasure of making a kill.

We waded through the mud and filth of the trenches and negotiated sandbagged positions located in apartment blocks overlooking the frontline. I looked into the bloodshot, vacant eyes of these men and realised that they were drained of all humanity and brutalised beyond belief.

I couldn't even begin to comprehend the frame of mind that allowed a man to place the crosshairs of his telescopic sight on the head of a small child, take up the trigger pressure with the pad of his forefinger, pause at the top of his breath, settle momentarily; and then, in that sweet moment of maximum stability between heartbeats, fire his weapon.

I could not imagine how such a man, seeing the child's head explode like a ripe melon, could then whoop in delight and high-five his comrades over his latest kill. I did not know how such a man could sleep at night.

But then, maybe he didn't.

CHAPTER 17

As renewed conflict between the Bosnians and the Serbs intensified, Lieutenant Harris surprised me one day by telling me that she had news about Katarina's father.

"He deserted from the Bosnian Army," she said. "About a year ago, when the Serbs were attacking Goražde."

"Why?"

"It's complicated. But basically, because he is a Serb."

I was astounded by this news, but then thought to myself that this explained the Madonna at his parent's farmhouse and the silver crucifix that his daughter had given me, which was secured around my neck. The Serbs were Orthodox Christians.

"He was a spy, then? Spying on the Bosnians?"

"No, of course not. There are quite a number of Serbs fighting with the Muslims." She could see I was confused. "Not every Serb wanted to see the collapse of Yugoslavia," she said.

"But why did he desert?"

"There was a lot of pressure on these people because of Serb ethnic cleansing. Somebody probably threatened to kill him. He decided to leave."

"So he's back on the dark side? The Serb side?"

The lieutenant shook her head. "They would kill him in a heartbeat. They'd see him as a traitor."

"Poor guy," I said.

"Yes."

"What about his family? They're Serbs then, stuck in Žepa? Why haven't they been run out by the Muslims?"

"Because everyone must know the family has someone serving in the Bosnian Army, that they're all fighting on the same side. And Žepa hasn't been so badly affected by the hatred and the ethnic cleansing."

"It's a little paradise."

"I expect it is," she said.

"You've not been there?"

"No."

I thought about this unexpected news for a few days, and as reports of the Serb attacks on the Muslim enclaves became increasingly worse, I began to see that Katarina's family must be in a very precarious situation.

If the population of Žepa started to take significant casualties, there was every possibility that the Muslims would start venting some of their anger on any Serb families that might still be there. But if Katarina's family tried to leave, or the enclave was overrun, their lives would be forfeit. The Serbs would kill them for sure.

I decided to tackle the lieutenant on this, so I pinned her down in a quiet corner of the Residency the next time I saw her. She looked pale and drawn, and I felt guilty at loading this on her. But I needed to try and do something.

"Oh sweetheart, I adore you for caring," she said. "But I don't see what can be done."

"Can't you speak with the general or something? The Ukrainians are still there. Couldn't they take care of the family? It is a UN safe zone, isn't it?"

"No darling, it's an unsafe zone." She was smiling at me, but her eyes were dark-rimmed and listless. "There's not much anyone can do, either for your friend's family or for anyone else. It seems like the Serbs intend taking the enclaves. Unless NATO or the Americans decide to go to war, everyone's lives are at risk."

"But you've been smuggling people across the confrontation lines. Couldn't you do it for these people too?" I asked.

"We're not running Schindler's List... Look, smuggling people through a few checkpoints around Sarajevo is pretty straightforward. Bringing them through remote roadblocks located in enemy-held territory would be a completely different prospect. It would end in tragedy."

I thought of how the major and I had been treated at Rogatica, and I knew she was right. "But there must be *something* we can do, Bella," I said. They're such a lovely family. Especially the girl... she has so much to live for. She wants to be a doctor, or an artist."

"You're so sweet. I can't help. But I do love you."

"Do you?" It was the first time she had said this.

"I'm crazy for you."

"You're gorgeous."

An artillery round exploded somewhere in the city.

"This is insane," said the lieutenant.

"It's getting closer to all-out war, isn't it?"

"I meant that our relationship is insane."

I wanted to hold her, kiss her, but she pushed me away.

"I'm sorry about your friends," she said. "You'll just have to wait and see how this all works out."

Then she was gone, and the following day I heard that she was working across on the dark side again.

So I worried about her and I worried about Katarina's family, and I worried about my leg too because the knee was swollen again and the pain was keeping me awake at nights.

The temperature climbed towards the height of summer whilst the great and the good debated the complexities of the Balkans issue and international news media editorials called for intervention; and the international community failed to find consensus and the United Nations Protection Force continued to bring in its humanitarian relief as best it could, whilst the Serbs laid their plans and the Bosnians tried to bring the Americans into the war on their side.

As the temperature rose, so too did the tension. The whole situation moved inexorably towards the promise of a looming, brooding tragedy. All of the entities were by now on a full war footing. Skirmishes and assaults were taking place in and around Sarajevo. Tensions along the Croatian border had erupted into full-scale warfare. In the east, the isolated Muslim pockets were on the verge of being overrun. The humanitarian mission ground to a near-halt.

Then Srebrenica fell.

We heard rumours of Serb-perpetrated abuse and atrocity. At first it was difficult to ascertain whether these rumours were just the product of the ever-efficient Bosnian propaganda machine. But with witness after witness appearing on television news broadcasts, it became increasingly apparent that there had indeed been a catastrophe.

I asked the warrant officer if the Observers had been reporting on this, for I knew that some of them were trapped with the Dutch in the Srebrenica enclave and that they had good communications. He told me that much of the rumour was true, but that I was to keep this to myself because the scale of what was going down was huge, and that the UN was very likely to be blamed for allowing it to happen. I thought this was ridiculous because we didn't even have enough firepower to force our way past road barriers and checkpoints manned by lightly equipped guards, let alone take on massed infantry supported by tanks and batteries of artillery.

But I was just a sergeant, and the world's most powerful politicians were pointing this finger so perhaps they could see something that I couldn't. Then I thought, well they're not here, in the heart of this thing, seeing the things that we were seeing, dealing with the ground truth realities that we had to deal with. So maybe my view was as cogent as theirs, or perhaps even more so.

Because when a soldier is given a mission, the mission needs to be achievable. His support and his equipment needs to be appropriate for the task at hand. But the United Nations Protection Force had *never* been equipped or even mandated to fight a war. It was simply not the mission. Blaming its soldiers, whether they were mighty generals or low-life like me, was utterly inappropriate.

We received reports suggesting that the Bosnian Serb Army may have summarily executed thousands of Muslims.

This was hard to absorb. Killed in follow-up military action, perhaps? But the reports were consistent, and it was certainly true that several thousand Muslims from Srebrenica were unaccounted for.

Refugees began to stream from the area; women, children and old men. But few men, if any, of a fighting age. The refugees told horrendous stories of abuse and rape, of murder by the roadside, of the enforced separation of families and the brutality of the Serb soldiers.

It was now clear that a tragedy of the first order was unfolding before us, the unleashing of an appalling bloodlust, the slaughter of countless men and a cruel humiliation of the innocent. Foresight had failed, and rabid dogs of war had been unleashed upon the people of Srebrenica.

We knew that Žepa was next.

As the rumours of savagery consolidated into fact, I began to fixate on the fate of Katarina and her family. I tried to share these concerns with others at the Residency, but everyone was too busy to pay any heed.

Lieutenant Harris returned from the Serb side looking more exhausted than ever. I tackled her again about Katarina's family. She told me to back off, that everything possible was being done to secure safe passage for the people of Žepa and that my friends were just a tiny part of a much bigger problem. She said that I'd made the mistake of becoming personally engaged, of allowing myself to care.

"It's no good," she said. "You have to let it go. If you don't, it will come to haunt you."

"Then why do you continue with all of this when your life is so much at risk?"

"Because I can't let it go."

"Why not?"

"I can't tell you. I *won't* tell you."

We were outside the Residency canteen and people were shoving past us. I thought, to hell with the politics of rank, and held her by the shoulders, forcing her to look at me.

"Why are you so driven by this place, Bella? Why don't you get out of here? Why don't *we* get out of here?"

"I can't... I don't..." She pulled away, pushed through the crush of incoming bodies, and I knew I couldn't reach her.

The warrant officer was by my side and he stopped me following her. "Come with me," he said, and it was an order.

The city was strangely quiet and I wondered if the sheer horror of the news from Srebrenica had stunned everybody into a state of shock. We drove to the old market of Baščaršija and found a small café that served decent Turkish coffee.

The warrant officer asked how much the lieutenant had told me about her first tour of duty in Bosnia, and I said not much. So he asked me if I'd like to know, and I said of course I would.

So he began by telling me he knew Bella and I were in love.

"It's that obvious?"

"It's an open secret."

"I thought we'd been discreet."

"She's been pretty good," he said. "But you're no spy, son."

"You're not the first person to tell me that."

The coffee arrived. It was thick and smelled delicious.

"Lieutenant Harris was here for almost a year," he said. "She had a pretty miserable time of it."

"I think it damaged her."

He took a sip of his coffee and nodded. "It damaged all of us. To a greater or lesser degree."

"You were here too?"

"I was, for some of the time. But not as long as Bella."

The coffee was good. The warrant officer offered me a cigarette and we lit up. The tobacco was harsh, but I drew it in deeply even though I'd been told to abstain because of the shrapnel wound to my lung.

"Were you based in Sarajevo?" I asked.

"Not me. She was, though, for a couple of months. Stayed here through the worst of the bombardments. It was a crazy time. Nobody could get in and nobody could get out."

"I thought most of the UN had withdrawn during all that?"

"Did I say she was working with the UN?"

"Oh. She did tell me a little about it," I said.

"When I next saw her, she was a bit shell-shocked," continued the warrant officer. "Turned out she'd been staying with a friend of hers in Sarajevo who was a staffer in the Bosnian Government. The woman's parents were killed in an artillery attack."

"I think we met. Her name's Almira, correct?"

He looked surprised. "Yes, that's the woman."

"I met her a couple of times with Bella, before Bagley was killed. She seemed a bit hard-nosed."

"Not surprising, is it?" said the warrant officer. "Losing your parents like that."

"I suppose not."

"Almira couldn't bring herself to identify the bodies, so Bella went instead. They'd been pretty much blown to bits and their remains scraped into a couple of bin-liners."

I thought of her sad look when she'd mentioned them. "She told me she knew them well," I said.

"Seeing people you know and love... it must have been devastating. You'd understand if you'd ever seen anything like it. You can never forget."

A NATO jet made a low pass over the city and terrified pigeons wheeled around the market stalls. The warrant officer signalled to the waiter for more coffee and lit another cigarette. We waited until the sound of the aircraft had faded into the distance.

"They should have sent her home," said the warrant officer, shaking his head. "Months later they sent her up towards Ahmici, where the Croats were ethnically cleansing Muslim families out of their homes and villages."

"I remember seeing that on the news."

"They didn't broadcast the worst of it, the images were too grim. Bella was right there. She saw things, things that no person should ever have to see. If her experiences in Sarajevo were grim, this was far, far worse. A hundred or more people dead, just in Ahmici. Bodies mutilated, houses burned down. Women and kids, whole families burned alive. It was appalling." He shifted uncomfortably on his chair. "You're right, it did damage her. She started buying-in to the tragedy of it all. She became personally engaged."

I couldn't even begin to imagine.

"Bella stuck with it, even though it affected her badly," he continued. "Always giving her best, always under pressure because she could speak the language. There's a lot to be admired in that woman. But you have to understand that she's deep. And maybe fractured to some degree. That will be a challenge, if you and she ever become an item. It might be wise not to become too involved."

We finished our coffee then drove back to the Residency.

I serviced the vehicle and prepared for whatever would come next. The sounds of conflict were escalating. The tragedy of Srebrenica was being played out. The fate of young Katarina's family hung in the balance as the Serbs began to move their artillery and their armour and their men towards the lightly defended enclave of Žepa.

I learned that Lieutenant Harris was on the dark side, helping negotiate safe passage for Žepa's civil population. I feared for her safety and I feared for the safety of Katarina's family.

I thought about the warrant officer's advice. Don't become involved he'd said. But it was far too late for that.

The news media berated the United Nations for its inadequacies and lack of will as we continued to drive our impossible mission forward against impossible odds, and in the face of all obstruction from the very people we were meant to be helping.

Then the humanitarian aid mission was suspended, the UN garrison from Goražde was withdrawn, and throughout the country we were ordered to adopt defensive positions in anticipation of God knew what. Everything had gravitated to one gigantic game of chess with nothing left on the board apart from pawns. Many of these were wearing blue berets.

But those most at risk, like young Katarina's family in Žepa, wore no uniform and carried no guns.

CHAPTER 18

The days rolled by, and the full scale of the Srebrenica disaster became apparent. Despite all denials from the Serb leadership it was obvious that a genocidal massacre of the enclave's male population had been enacted in the hills and the fields of that beautiful region.

We received word that the Bosnian Serb Army had Žepa surrounded and isolated. It appeared there was nothing that could be done to prevent the enclave being overwhelmed. A second humanitarian tragedy seemed inevitable as the Serbs started shelling the town.

Then the general announced that its civil population was to be evacuated under the protection of the UN, that he had personally negotiated this with the Serb military leadership and that the operation would begin immediately.

Suddenly I was elated and excited at the prospect of Katarina's family making it safely to one of the refugee camps or even into Sarajevo. As the evacuation ground into gear, I found myself hovering around the door of our Belgian colleagues who had responsibility for coordinating convoy movements across the country. But detailed information was sparse. All we knew was that trucks and buses were transporting thousands of locals towards refugee camps or holding areas that were a long way from Sarajevo.

We spoke with some Norwegians at a refugee camp near the town of Zenica, and they confirmed that women, children and old men were arriving. Hope began to rise that maybe the Serbs by now had done enough killing and raping and dehumanising. Lists of names began to filter in, but there was no mention of Katarina's family.

Lieutenant Harris returned. She was filthy and exhausted, and I was horrified at her condition. Her eyes were red-rimmed and her complexion was almost death-like. She tried to eat, but it made her feel sick. I persuaded her to hydrate, but after a glass or two of water she retched it up onto the floor.

I coerced some precious lime cordial from the cooks and sat with her as she took small sips between puffing nervously on her cigarettes. I asked if she had any way of checking on the fate of Katarina's family.

"We'll know soon enough," she said. "The Red Cross is involved. They're very good at compiling the statistics. Maybe you should go and ask them."

"You're exhausted," I said. "Are you going to get some rest?"

She lay her head on my shoulder, and we no longer cared about rank or protocol or career, or even the Queen's Regulations. "Like this?" she asked.

I hugged her, thinking all the time that she had become very thin and that if anyone deserved a medal, it was her.

"When are you out again?" I asked.

"Who knows? Today? Tomorrow? Ten minutes from now?"

"It's too much."

"It's barely enough." She shuddered. "I have to get some sleep."

We walked to her cabin. She opened the door and unexpectedly pulled me inside. It was empty apart from the two of us.

"Bella…"

"Shhh." She slumped down on her bunk. I sat alongside her and we held hands. "If anything happens to me, please tell my mother…" She paused.

"Tell your mother what?"

"That I tried. I really tried."

"You try too hard."

"I do, don't I?"

"Yes you do, sweet Bella. By God, you try far too hard."

She smiled and for a moment there was a wonderful brightness in her tired grey eyes. Then she lay back with all her clothes on, and in a moment was fast asleep.

I stayed for a while, looking at her exhausted face as it relaxed into a deeper level of unconsciousness. I waited until her breathing became deep and steady, then gently disengaged my hands, kissed her lightly on the forehead, turned off her light and left.

The next morning, I drove out with the warrant officer to the Red Cross headquarters in Sarajevo, but they had no news. They were clearly overwhelmed by the scale of what had been happening in the eastern enclaves, and other parts of the country where tragedy was being played out on a numbing scale. The insanity of war had prevailed, and the slide towards a resumption of full-scale hostilities appeared to be unstoppable.

The civil population of the city had taken once more to their cellars, remaining indoors throughout most of the day and only venturing out when darkness began to fall and the snipers had less chance of scoring a kill. UN troops were now being regularly shot at. Movement around the city was being severely restricted by the French. The Serbs had sealed us in, and their leadership was screaming blue murder at the Secretary General because they believed that the United Nations and the Americans had come into the war on the side of the Muslims.

Still there was no word of Katarina's family. Despite his wise advice, the warrant officer appeared to have bought-in to the idea of caring about their fate. Perhaps he had been influenced by my concern, though I'd taken him to be a hard-bitten old soldier who'd seen too much and done too much to care.

We checked with the Red Cross almost every day and even managed to liaise with the Ukrainians as they withdrew from Žepa, but they had no news either. The Serbs had occupied the enclave. We heard from the Norwegians at Zenica that refugees from Žepa were generally reporting good treatment during their evacuation, though many had been traumatised at the sheer terror of not knowing their ultimate fate as they drove away under the guns of the Bosnian Serb Army.

"We may hear nothing," said the warrant officer. "I can't see the Serbs allowing the UN back into Žepa anytime soon."

"I'll stay in touch with the Red Cross," I said.

"Might be a forlorn hope."

"Better than no hope."

Lieutenant Harris was out and about again, sometimes working with the general, sometimes liaising with the French, sometimes down at the Bosnian Presidency. She had become gaunt and distant, a shadow of the vibrant woman I'd first met during the autumn. I couldn't get close to her, and I longed for us to be free of this place with its depressing gloom, its sniping and its bombing, its endless tragedy and eternal despair.

The appalling story of Srebrenica appeared to be changing the international political landscape. The United Nations mission was collapsing, and the prospect of being precipitated into a war against the Bosnian Serbs was staring us in the face.

There was much talk in the news media about the prospects of an American-led NATO deployment into the country if a peace accord could be secured between the warring factions. In anticipation of this, the Observers were now scouting locations around Sarajevo that might be used for the basing of NATO troops.

Early one evening I drove with the warrant officer to check out a complex on the western edge of the city that was being slated for use if NATO did deploy. The complex sat on the Serb side of the confrontation line, but by now all movements across to the dark side had been stopped.

"Don't fancy being arrested as a spy anyway," growled the warrant officer as we drove along Sniper Alley. A couple of bullets cracked by, but by now we hardly considered this to be effective enemy fire so we didn't take evasive action. "We'll get as close as we can on the Muslim side and try to get eyes-on the complex," he said.

We negotiated our way through the suburb of Rajlovac. The closer we got to the confrontation line, the rougher became the neighbourhood. Then, turning a sharp corner, we ran into a Bosnian checkpoint manned by a handful of Muslim soldiers who were surprised to see a UN vehicle in this area. But the warrant officer was quick off the mark, producing a carton of cigarettes and a bottle of *Slivovica*. Within a few minutes an English-speaking sergeant had climbed into the vehicle with us and, with the promise of further reward if he could help out, was guiding us downhill towards a thin winding river that marked the boundary between the warring factions.

"It is difficult to get close," said the soldier. "And we have to be careful. The Serbs always open fire when they see us."

We left the Land Rover at the edge of the built-up area and continued downhill on foot. The ground was uneven and covered with head-high scrub.

"We must get low," said our guide, pointing out a red roof on the far side of the river. "The Serbs have men watching from beneath the roof tiles."

We shuffled forward on all fours, and after another fifty metres or so I began to notice spent bullets and rusting barbed wire, interspersed with half-empty sandbags that had been torn apart by gunfire.

And then I noticed bones, *human bones*, that had been bleached white in the summer sun, sticking out of the ground, spread along a combat line that must have seen furious fighting.

"This will do," I said, grabbing our guide by his leg.

"It's OK," he said, grinning broadly. "You wait here with your friend, I will go ahead and check. There's a great view from over there." He was pointing towards the burned-out hulk of an armoured personnel carrier that was abandoned and covered with rust. He was off again before we could say anything.

"This is a bit fucked-up," I said.

"Would be good to get a better view," said the warrant officer, shrugging his shoulders.

A few minutes later the young soldier was headed back in a doubled-over shuffling run giving us a thumbs-up. Then there was a dull crump and the force of an explosion slammed into me in that horribly familiar way. I saw our guide describe a perfect somersault and come back to earth in a crumpled heap. Stones and dirt rained down upon us. A cloud of black smoke curled towards the evening sky and the smell of cordite was sharp in my nose.

Then the boy was screaming, clawing at the stump of his leg, hands covered in blood; and the warrant officer was running towards him and I was thinking *we're in the middle of a bloody minefield*; and then I was running towards the boy too, grabbing the shattered remains of his leg and pushing his convulsing body towards the ground.

The Serbs opened fire.

"Get your belt around his leg," said the warrant officer. It was an order, not a request. He was pressing his thumbs hard into the boy's groin, seeking the femoral pressure point, trying to staunch the flow of blood.

I looked at the end of the stump. The severed tendons were twitching and it was squirting with an arterial bleed. The bone was shattered and torn flesh hung down, the shredded skin blackened and bruised. I unbuckled my belt. My holstered pistol fell to the ground. I passed the belt around the boy's thigh.

"As tight as you can," said the warrant officer, urgently.

I heaved it in and locked it off. I was vaguely aware of bullets cracking all around. I figured that the Serbs couldn't see us otherwise we'd have been dead by now.

The boy's screams were becoming breathless. Bright, frothy blood was issuing from his mouth and nose. The warrant officer held him down, ripped off his combat jacket, exposed his chest. Multiple puncture wounds under the boy's ribs oozed dark blood.

"Shrapnel in his lungs," said the warrant officer. "His liver, too."

He boy's hand grabbed my arm, fingers digging hard.

"Please... please..."

"It's OK, try to relax..."

"No, no..."

He was clawing at my side, searching. I tried to force him back, make him relax. The belt slipped from his thigh. Blood began pumping again. The warrant officer was back on the pressure point.

"Get the belt..."

The boy twisted to one side and let go an ear-piercing scream. I could see his spine had been partially severed. His hand clawed at the warrant officer. Closed on his gun, tried to pull it free. I twisted him away and he screamed again, splattering my jacket with blood and spit.

"Please... shoot me... please..."

"The belt! Get the fucking belt!"

My hands were shaking. This was crazy, unreal. The boy wanted to die. He wanted us to shoot him.

I fumbled with the belt. Bullets were cracking over our heads. Any moment now the Serbs were going to get their range, nail us.

The boy was bleeding and this was a minefield. We were going to die here and now, in this place, with this kid, on the Serb frontline.

There was my gun, at my feet, still in its holster. The boy saw it, reached for it... couldn't reach it...

"Please, please..."

His eyes bored into mine, pleading, crazed. He wanted to die. I didn't want to die. The Serbs would kill us. I didn't want the Serbs to kill us. The boy was dying.

The boy wants to die.

The iron-hard reality of the moment settled on me and stilled my mind. I dropped the belt and picked up my gun. It was a Sig P226, 9mm. I cocked the action and lined up the shot. The pistol was cold and hard in my hand.

I had never killed anyone before. I could see Bagley's face. I didn't want to die. I didn't want the boy to die. But the boy wanted to die. My foresight settled on his forehead.

"Please..."

I took up the pressure. Anticipated the shot, half-closed my eyes...

A burst of automatic gunfire from behind me ripped into the boy's torso. He crumpled. I spun. One of his colleagues was stood there, slinging his rifle. He brushed me aside and began to gather the boy's bleeding corpse.

"Help," he said.

So we half-carried, half-dragged the body whilst the Serbs continued to fire randomly in our general direction and a couple of mortar rounds exploded too far distant to matter. We reached the edge of the built-up area and dropped the boy's body to the ground. The soldier stared at us coldly and we left.

I tried not to vomit. The warrant officer squeezed my shoulder. He didn't need to say a thing.

CHAPTER 19

We were halfway back to the Residency when the woman stepped right out in front of us. There was no chance to avoid the impact. She bounced off the wing of the Land Rover and spun to the ground as the warrant officer slammed on the brakes and brought us to a shuddering halt. She was struggling to stand when I reached her. I forced her to stay on the ground.

"Is OK..." she said.

"No, you must stay still, you could make things worse by moving."

"Is OK... is OK..."

The warrant officer was on the radio to our operations room, calling for help. The woman had stopped struggling and was sat in the gutter trying to gather the contents of her bag which were strewn around the road; a half loaf of bread, a tin of vegetables, a few medications and a broken bottle of orange cordial.

I could see that the palms of her hands were grazed. Blood was seeping through her thick woollen stockings around her knees. She was not young, probably in her seventies, but her eyes were bright blue and clear.

"They're sending someone with a medical kit," said the warrant officer. "How is she?"

"Not keen on accepting help," I said.

"Tough old bird, huh?"

Nobody offered to help. We were at a junction notorious for sniper shootings, so maybe that was understandable. We gathered the woman's things and I tried to take a look at her leg, but she pushed my hands away. She tried again to stand, so we helped her and it was clear nothing was broken. It must have been a glancing blow. She tried to walk, but sank again to the ground.

"Where do you live?" I asked.

"Is OK."

This seemed to be the extent of her English vocabulary.

Another Land Rover pulled up alongside us. It was Lieutenant Harris, and she had a first aid kit.

"I was at the Red Cross headquarters," she said, kneeling beside the woman.

"Couldn't they send a medic?" I asked.

"It's not that kind of place. Not a hospital or a clinic, I mean."

The lieutenant spoke to the woman, checked her bloodied hands and felt along her damaged leg. I was hoping the Serb snipers were taking a smoke break or playing cards. Or that today's sweepstake didn't include little old ladies sat by the road in pain.

"She wants us to take her home."

"Why not to the hospital?" asked the warrant officer. "She needs to get those injuries properly seen to."

"Let's just take her home," said the lieutenant and it sounded like an order.

The warrant officer shrugged. "Where does she live?"

"Nearby. Overlooking Sniper Alley."

We loaded the woman into the lieutenant's Land Rover, then convoyed slowly along the main road and pulled in behind an austere-looking apartment block whose frontal façade had been shattered by two years of interminable sniper fire. Not shattered in the sense of being utterly destroyed like many of the buildings in Grbavica or Dobrinja, but every window had been shot out and then covered over with a patchwork mix of plastic sheeting, cardboard and plywood.

We carried the old woman up several flights of stairs and into her apartment. The place was simply furnished, and I could see in a moment why she didn't want to be taken to the hospital, didn't want any kind of a fuss. A picture of the Pope was hung on the living room wall, and there was a small altar complete with an effigy of Our Blessed Lady in the corner. The woman must have been Catholic, a Bosnian Croat.

I asked the lieutenant if this was the case, but she corrected me. "Not a Bosnian Croat," she said. "This woman and her husband are from Croatia."

I had no idea if this was better or worse. But just as I was about to ask, the bedroom door opened and there stood an old man. He was thin, stooped, and was wearing old string vest over his pyjama trousers.

"Hello, you are most welcome," he said. His words were laboured and his breath was short, but his English was clear. "I see you have returned my dear wife to me."

Predrag Jurić and his wife had been living in Sarajevo since long before the beginning of the Balkans crisis. He was suffering from emphysema. Given his shortness of breath and generally poor state of health, I couldn't help thinking that his journey was almost done.

His wife, by contrast, was a ball of energy and far from spent. Lieutenant Harris cleaned her hands and bandaged her leg. Then the old girl was up and about, fussing around the place, boiling water on a small electric stove and slicing up the half-loaf we'd recovered from the road.

Predrag Jurić parked himself at a small kitchen table and we joined him. He was articulate and apparently delighted at the unexpected company.

"Isn't it dangerous for you to be here in Sarajevo?" I asked. "As a Croatian?"

"Not so much," he said. He spoke slowly and carefully, each intake of breath sounding like mucus sucked through a straw. "In the early days, maybe, and during the fighting between the Muslims and the Croats, particularly so. But last year we had the ceasefire. And now, the Federation."

"The Federation between the Muslims and the Croats," explained the lieutenant. "They decided between them that the Serbs were the common enemy."

"So now my wife and I are not really at risk," continued Predrag. "But we still keep ourselves to ourselves. It's probably safer that way."

His wife gave us all a cup of steaming hot tea that was weak but lightly flavoured with lemon, then put a plate of sliced bread thinly smeared with apricot jam in the middle of the table. We thanked her, and she said "OK, OK," then proceeded to hobble around the apartment straightening furniture, tidying things away and flicking a threadbare rag at the dust.

A bare lightbulb swung above our heads, casting ill-defined shadows across the table and onto the walls. Daylight was beginning to fade, and I could hear early volleys of rifle shots crackling across the warring divide.

"These people," said Predrag. "Always they shoot, always they fight. It is tiresome."

"Can't you move house?" I asked. "You're very exposed here. Almost on the front line."

"We've lived here for twenty years," he said. "And now I have the disease. What can we do? We live here and I shall die here. It is of no consequence."

His wife walked past us, flicking with her cloth, and said something. Both Predrag and the lieutenant laughed.

"She says the Serbs are rotten shots," said Isabella. "Says they shoot all night and never hit a thing, that maybe the UN should teach them how to shoot properly."

I looked at the shattered remains of the windows and had already noticed several strike marks on the apartment's internal walls, some of them very close to where we were sitting. I supposed it was really just a roll of the dice whether the old boy or his wife got shot. I remembered the lieutenant telling me that the distances were so great that the snipers were more likely to miss than hit. But this place did seem so very much closer to the confrontation line than where we were stood when she gave me that wise advice.

"Bosnia must be very hard for you people to understand," said Predrag. The warrant officer reassured him that this was so, using an expletive not intended for delicate ears. "It has always been this way," continued the old man. "Even during the war, with the Axis powers to contend with. We couldn't bear to fight alongside each other."

"The second world war?" I asked. "You fought in the second world war?"

"How could I not?"

"You don't look old enough," I said.

"Thank you. I was very young."

"Who did you fight with?"

"I'm a Croatian. Most of us fought with the Ustaše."

The lieutenant could see the puzzled look on my face. "The Ustaše was a fascist movement that euthanised hundreds of thousands of Serbs," she said. "And Jews, and others."

I looked at this tiny man sat in his raggedy pyjamas and torn string vest. "You were a fascist?" I asked.

He gave me a hard, searching stare, then said "I didn't say that *I* fought with the Ustaše."

"Then with who?"

"I fought alongside Tito, with the Partisans. I never conformed to the fascist ideal. Many of us didn't. But it was a roll of the dice, a big gamble. If the Nazis had won, we'd all have been killed."

"But they didn't win."

"No. Tito came to power. The Partisans took the prize, supported by the British. Then Tito butchered the Ustaše and the Četniks, who were the Royalist Serbs. Or at least, the leaderships and those that couldn't get away."

"Good call, then," I said. "Fighting with the Partisans."

"The gamble paid off. It was a civil war, really. The Partisans against the Ustaše and everyone against the Četniks. And now, we have this."

The night was drawing-in fast, and the weight of sniper fire outside was intensifying. There was a loud bang as an explosive-headed round impacted close-by the apartment's window. I flinched, but Predrag remained impassive. The light swung gently above our heads. His wife was at the window, looking out towards the Serb lines as if to see where the sniper fire was coming from.

Then the lieutenant's foot touched mine, and suddenly we were holding hands under the table. It seemed like forever since we'd been close and I glanced at her face. But she was intent on maintaining the façade, even at this late hour, even though the warrant officer knew.

"Who takes care of your medical condition?" I asked.

"My wife's cousin works at the hospital. She takes care of things. There is always a way."

"You can't risk going there yourself?"

"There have been incidents," said Predrag. "People have been dragged out from there by the Bosniaks."

"From the hospital?"

"This is what we hear. It is better not to take the chance."

The sniper fire grew more intense. Green flashes from passing tracer rounds silhouetted Predrag's wife momentarily as she stared out of the shattered window.

The warrant officer had been listening to all of this with his eyes narrowed and his jaw clenched.

"A boy stood on a landmine today," he said, abruptly. "Had his leg blown off. He wanted us to kill him. We were going to kill him. The Sergeant here had his gun out, was going to shoot him in the head. I was going to stop him and do it myself. But the boy's friend did it instead."

I could feel Isabella's hand tightening on mine.

"Where is the sense in it all?" continued the warrant officer. "Where's the sense in you people hating each other so much? Where's the sense in us coming over here to help you, and seeing stuff, and doing stuff, and shooting young kids in the head because they've stood on a fucking landmine? Where is the sense in it?"

The old boy's face neither hardened nor softened. The sniper fire redoubled in its intensity. More rounds impacted the wall. The light swung above our heads. The old woman stared out of the window. In the yellow light of the bare electric bulb I could see veins standing out on the warrant officer's temples.

"You see, there is a problem with these people," said Predrag, gently. "It is a question of attitude."

A bullet came into the apartment, smacking into the living room wall and sending a shower of plaster and wood across the threadbare carpet. I joined the warrant officer on the floor, but neither the lieutenant nor the old man moved an inch. We righted our chairs and rejoined them at the table, sheepishly. The old woman stared out of the window, close to the fresh bullet hole.

"You see, we did not flinch," said Predrag, gesturing towards Isabella and his wife.

"Yes, I can see that," I said.

"What do you mean by a question of attitude?" asked the warrant officer, his anger spent.

The old man reached for a slice of bread, took a bite and chewed on it thoughtfully for a moment. The bulb swung and the sniper fire continued. I realised we were showing a light. It must be attracting incoming fire. My heart was racing. The lieutenant took my hand once more, squeezing it tightly.

"They kill us. We kill them," said Predrag. "We all kill each other. It has always been this way. These people want to avenge the dead, reclaim their land and the bones of their ancestors. It is as much a war about the dead as a war about the living."

"But that's insane," I said. "The world has to move on. Everyone has to move on."

"It's not so simple," said Isabella. "These hatreds run deep. And memories are long."

"So now we have another round of the old enmities," continued Predrag. "Another generation where memories of death and destruction will prevail for a lifetime. It's as if this region is cursed, that it can never let go of the past."

"So we should just leave and let you all get on with it?" asked the warrant officer, and I thought it was a reasonable question.

"You must do what you think it right," replied the old man. "But one thing I can tell you for sure." He paused as a renewed intensity of sniper fire peppered the building, then leant forward, drilling me with his watery grey eyes. "There can be no hope for Bosnia when people lose respect for themselves. When that happens, men will do anything. All the rules crumble to dust. And then nothing matters apart from hatred and revenge, and death."

Another round smashed into the apartment, embedding itself in the kitchen wall close to where we were sat. Uncomfortably close, dangerously close. This time I resisted the urge to disappear under the table.

Predrag Jurić held my eyes with his unblinking stare.

"Do you think we should switch off the light?" I asked.

There was a momentary pause.

"This would be a very good idea," he said.

The old man reached up and pulled the cord.

We sat in darkness for several minutes without speaking as the sniper fire diminished and night closed in.

CHAPTER 20

The major didn't seem much pleased with the results of our reconnaissance task, and had no interest in why we didn't get close enough to gain a good view of the hotel complex. I thought for a moment that the warrant officer was going to punch him, but military discipline prevailed and instead we headed for the canteen and scratched around for a late supper.

I could not believe how slowly things seemed to be moving. There was a tension in the air that threatened some kind of catastrophe, yet the international community prevaricated and the United Nations soldiers on the ground had little to do except harden their fortifications and wonder what would come next. The humanitarian mission seemed to be entirely stalled.

Stories that had emerged from Srebrenica and its aftermath were horrendous. I lay awake on my bunk for much of that night and wondered yet again what had become of young Katarina and her family.

It did seem that the vast majority of people from Žepa had been safely evacuated. Most of the men, having learned the fate of their comrades in Srebrenica, had taken to the woods before the Serbs tightened their grip around the enclave. Some refugees from Žepa had made it into Sarajevo. I resolved to check once again with the Red Cross to see if there was any news.

The next morning at breakfast Lieutenant Harris sat beside me. Her eyes were bloodshot and circled with dark rings. I asked if she managed to get much sleep, but she too had spent much of the night awake, wondering what would come next. I told her I'd be visiting the Red Cross again to ask about Katarina's family.

"I'll come with you," she said. "Though I did ask when I was there yesterday, and they still couldn't help."

We drove through the city, which was calm and relatively quiet. I could hear the occasional distant explosion and the sporadic rat-a-tat of machine gun fire, but at a lower intensity than usual.

I watched the lieutenant as she drove, and could see that she was biting at her lower lip. I still didn't know the full extent of what she had been involved in these past few weeks, and I knew that she wouldn't tell me. I wondered if she was part of the Intelligence community, or if she really was a Serb spy. Or if she was just a well-meaning young officer who consistently put duty before self, to the point of self-destruction.

"What will you do when we're finished here?" I asked.

"I don't know. Go back to my unit, I suppose."

"You really think you'll stay in the Army?"

"Probably. Maybe." She bit at the shredded remains of her fingernails. "Who knows? How about you?"

"I don't see this as a career. It's more an experience."

"One you'd rather forget?"

"Probably."

"I said you'd get to know this place if you stuck around. A disaster around every corner."

I reached up and pulled her hand away from her mouth. She glanced at me, and gave a tired smile.

"And what about us, darling?" she asked. "What do you think about us?"

"I think we need some quality time together," I replied.

"Here? In this place?"

"After. In any place."

"You're sweet."

"No I'm not, Bella. I'm in love."

She looked at me again and for a fleeting moment there was real warmth in her sad grey eyes, but she didn't respond.

The people at the International Committee of the Red Cross were polite, but once again dismissive. They were dealing with tens of thousands of refugees, they said, and though they understood our friends were important to us, we just needed to be patient. Lists were being compiled, and we could be sure that any news, good or bad, would eventually be forthcoming. It was obvious that they wanted us to quit bothering them. I resolved to leave them in peace for a week.

We departed, and I asked Isabella if we could stop at the Old Town for coffee. We parked up in a crowded side street and walked towards the open air market a short distance away. The lieutenant slipped her arm through mine, and suddenly I felt relaxed and happy because she was a wonderful person and we'd had so little time in each other's company these past few weeks.

"I'll be glad when we're finished here," I said. "It's so grey, so miserable."

"That's the war. Sarajevo was a wonderfully cosmopolitan city before all this. It was culturally alive, exciting. So many artists, so many writers and musicians."

"All I see is sorrow, hatred and death."

"Same as any other city at war, then."

I supposed this was true.

We stopped at a small café and drank strong Turkish coffee washed down with lukewarm water.

"Do you feel hungry?" I asked.

"I always feel hungry."

"Then let's eat."

"I'd rather not."

"Why?"

"Nothing ever tastes good." She lit a cigarette.

"I wish you wouldn't, Bella," I said.

"Why not?"

"You should eat instead."

She smiled at me and stubbed out her cigarette. "Then let's grab something."

The waiter brought us two *ćevapi* sandwiches that were small but delicious, though I did wonder what kind of meat was in the sausage. I wolfed mine down, but Isabella nibbled without energy so I ended up eating half of hers too rather than allowing it to go to waste. We drank a second coffee, and I decided I wanted a *džezva* coffee pot to take home as a souvenir. So I suggested we walk along to the market to pick one up.

The streets were busy, with battered old cars sounding their horns and people scurrying to and fro clutching bags of vegetables or whatever goods were on offer. There was a curious energy about the place, as if people were somehow feeling guilty that they had money to spend. Or maybe they were just keen to get their shopping done whist it was quiet and then head back to the safety of their homes.

The lieutenant took my arm again and squeezed hard. It seemed so incongruous in a city filled with so much pain and sorrow and bitterness to feel love in my heart. But I did, I truly did. If I could just find a way of getting Bella away from here, everything would be fine. The current crisis would reach its resolution. Then we'd find a reason to take a liaison trip somewhere, to Zagreb maybe, or down to the coast. There must be a way. We'd find a way. We had to find a way.

We were just a few steps short of the turn when a series of massive explosions knocked us off our feet and glass came raining down.

I rolled on top of the lieutenant, shielding her, protecting her from the glass and small chunks of masonry and roof tiles and debris. Something sliced my ear, and I had blood; but not streams of blood, just a small nick and we were otherwise unhurt.

Then there was dust and screaming and shouting, and people running away and people running towards; and cars reversing along the street ahead, and more screaming and shouting, guttural screams, screams of agony and of fear; and then voices shouting in panic and hysteria.

We picked ourselves up and ran to the corner.

Before us lay a scene of ruin; a scene of butchery and death, a scene of human suffering on a scale beyond imagination and beyond all reason.

Isabella slumped against a wall but I stumbled on into the heart of carnage. Everything I had seen before, everything I had felt before, paled into utter insignificance at the sheer brutality of it.

I walked amongst the mortal remains of innocent people savagely slaughtered; heads decapitated, limbs torn off, blood flowing freely. People without legs were clawing their way across the ground, dragging the remains of their mutilated bodies with them. Others lay there, crying for help, arms outstretched, eyes wide with shock and horror.

Locals were running in from all sides, men with cigarettes hanging from the sides of their mouths, women still carrying their bags of shopping. The body of a young man lay sprawled across a traffic barrier, a massive hole blown in the side of his chest. Other bodies, shapeless, shattered and torn, lay scattered around as if thrown by some gigantic hand in a fit of barbaric rage.

I reached down to a man who was twitching in the gutter, but his brain had been blown completely through the side of his skull. Congealing blood pooled in craters. My boots slipped and slithered amongst ruptured, pulsating intestines that were oozing faecal matter.

Cars were sounding their horns. I turned back. There was no sign of Bella. Bile was rising in my throat. I tried to call her name, but nothing. Panic started to overtake me. Men were loading the injured, many of them mortally injured, into the trunks of cars. They were shouting and screaming, dragging the wounded, pulling at the limbs of the dead.

I should have helped; it was my duty to help.

I could not help.

This was beyond my experience, beyond my training, beyond anything I ever imagined I would see. Where was Bella? Where was sense and reason? Where the fuck was humanity?

Where was Bella?

Then I saw her, kneeling in the debris and the blood, head buried in her hands. I ran to her, took her by the shoulders, turned her face towards mine.

But her eyes were glazed over and there was no recognition. Just the wide, staring look of a dislocated mind.

She was mouthing silent words and her whole frame was trembling like a fragile leaf in an autumn wind.

I knew in that instant that I had lost her.

I lifted her bodily and carried her away like a broken child. My tears fell onto her hair and my feet stumbled across the ground.

CHAPTER 21

Lieutenant Harris took to her bunk in the Residency, curled into a foetal position with her head turned to the wall.

There was little to be done for her. The warrant officer was sympathetic, but as of now the entire United Nations Protection Force was under orders to consolidate in secure areas. It was clear that something of immense significance was looming over us. It was as if the marketplace attack was galvanising the international community to finally come down off its fence and become directly involved.

In common with so many other atrocities perpetrated on the civil population of Sarajevo, there were persistent rumours that the Muslims may have been responsible for killing their own citizens in order to demonise the Serbs, to force NATO and the Americans to come in on their side.

The general determined to send a fact-finding team from his headquarters to investigate, and I was slated to drive one of the vehicles.

I didn't want to go, didn't want to leave Isabella. But everything was spinning. Officers were running around and the NATO Air Liaison Cell next to our office was a hive of frantic energy, so I really didn't have any choice.

I tried to have someone commit to watching over her, but nobody was interested. She was yesterday's news. It was time to gear-up for warfighting, or whatever was next on the menu in this sorry place. An opportunity for bravery and heroism and medals and stuff, a time to shine.

I had just enough time to check in on her, give her a kiss and tell her I'd be back soon. Then I was off and away with the warrant officer, leading a convoy of the brave towards a scene of tragedy and despair.

It was almost as if we needn't have bothered. The French had the area tightly cordoned off, and we had a tough time convincing them to let us through. But they eventually did, and I could feel my heart racing as we approached the marketplace. Or rather, the streets close-by the marketplace, for in truth the attack had found its mark a short distance along the main street to the west. We parked-up and walked the last hundred yards or so.

When we got there I was astonished to see that evidence of the carnage had already been largely cleared away. French soldiers were measuring distances from a series of strike marks on the road to shrapnel holes in nearby walls, taking bearings on their prismatic compasses and trying to ascertain the direction from which the fire must have come. Locals were hosing away blood and scrubbing at the ground. Others were sweeping up glass and debris into piles ready to be carted off.

The officers from the Residency wandered around, taking pictures and stopping occasionally to talk with the French soldiers. The warrant officer was taking notes of his own which I imagined would be passed up the British chain of command. For a moment I thought he wanted me to take a photograph of him with the whole panorama of trauma and death set out behind, but he saw the look of distaste on my face and thought better of it.

There was a tug at my sleeve. An old woman was stood there with a brush in one hand and her other held out towards me.

"Cigarette?" she asked. I offered her one and she took it with trembling fingers. "Match?"

"You speak English?"

"Match? Thank you. Thank you."

I pulled out a lighter, and could see my hands were trembling just as much as hers. I cupped the flame and she drew deeply.

"Thank you. Thank you." She looked into my face. Her eyes were hooded and dark, empty of emotion and devoid of hope. "Bad men," she said, shaking her head. "Bad men." She turned away with the cigarette hanging loosely from the side of her mouth and continued with her task of sweeping bloodied glass from the pavement.

I walked to a street corner and leaned against a wall. Lit up a smoke of my own and watched the scene play out.

Blue helmets and green flak jackets, white armoured personnel carriers and the shambles of war. Water was running down the road, mixed with blood and dust. Some of it had pooled in a small crater and shrapnel splash marks on the road close beside me. The blood was reflecting the light of day, giving the curious impression of a bright red, multi-petalled flower. It was almost beautiful, and in sharp contrast to the many shades of grey that dominated the scene.

The warrant officer walked across and told me that upwards of forty people had been killed and dozens more injured. I pointed out the flower to him. He told me that this was not uncommon in the city, and they were known as roses, Sarajevo roses; and I knew I would never be able to look at a rose again without thinking of this place.

We loaded into our vehicle and led the convoy back to the Residency in silence.

Lieutenant Harris was still lying on her bunk, but she was awake and smiled at me thinly when I came into the room.

"Did I make a fool of myself?" she asked. Her voice was as thin as her lips.

"Of course not," I said. "It was just overwhelming."

"Yes. Do you have a cigarette?"

"I shall get you some soup."

"I'd prefer a cigarette."

"Then you shall have both."

I returned a short time later, but she was sleeping so I set the soup on a small table, kissed her head and closed the door gently as I left.

The rest of the day passed in something of a blur. The evening drew in, and unusually there was very little sound of gunfire across Sniper Alley or from other parts of the front line. It was as if this latest catastrophe had stunned the situation into hiatus and silenced the guns.

We knew that the news media had been whipped into a frenzy of protest and scorn at the uselessness of the UN, and that there were now widespread calls for intervention. The Bosnian Presidency was playing to this for all it was worth. And who could blame them, I thought, with a river of Muslim blood on the streets?

The French investigation had proved inconclusive, but the balance of probability was that the mortar attack – for we now knew that the market area had been struck by several mortar rounds – was the work of the Serbs. One more Serb atrocity piled on a mountain of atrocities inflicted upon the largely defenceless population of this city.

The following day was full of rumour and counter-rumour. It was a day of politics and promises, a day during which the world seemed to hold its breath. In the midst of this, amongst the planning and the talking and a gradual return to arms by the snipers on the line, I held Bella when I could and took turn and about on watch from within the fortified walls of our compound with its outlook across the adjacent park.

And then a young girl collecting firewood died before my eyes, shot through the head by a sniper.

So I wept, and I fell from the partial divide; yearning with every fibre of my being for something to be done against the bastard Serbs and their bastard guns and the fucked-up mentality that allowed them to kill an innocent child.

And at last I came to understand this place, for a coldness settled upon my heart and bitter hatred welled within my breast. Everything was telling me that men who inflict such crimes needed to die like dogs; and I knew that I could kill such men in cold blood, outside the boundaries of law and with my bare hands, were I to be given the chance.

I knew that I could do this, and without shame.

CHAPTER 22

We were on full alert when the bombing began, though quite who we were meant to be on alert against in the heart of Sarajevo eluded me.

NATO was bombing Serb positions all around the city, targeting their communications system, heavy weapons concentrations, and their command and control infrastructure. As a demonstration of shock and awe, it was impressive. The night sky was lit with a constant barrage of bright flashes and huge fireballs as some installation or another was struck with unerring accuracy.

The noise was terrific. Each blast sent shockwaves across the city that rocked the Residency and rattled its windows despite the shatterproof taping. Artillery from the UNPROFOR Rapid Reaction Corps opened up from the slopes of Mount Igman, raining fire down upon Serb positions wherever they presented a danger to UN troops. It was now transparently obvious that NATO and the US and the UN had decided to attack the Serbs in force.

Lieutenant Harris managed to claw her way into the Residency canteen, but she didn't stay long. I followed her back to her accommodation and was shocked at how she seemed to have aged. It was like following an old woman. She clearly needed help, but where was help to be had in this place?

"I need to get you out of here," I said, sitting alongside her on her bunk. "You need to see a doctor."

She nodded, then rested her head on my shoulder. I could feel her wince with every new explosion. Every last ounce of the supreme confidence she had shown the day we walked along that ridge overlooking the city, when the snipers were firing at us, had totally disappeared. The contrast could not be more extreme.

So it must be with a fractured mind, I thought. She must have been walking on the edge, staring into the void. And finally she'd fallen, her nerve gone, her courage spent.

Hell, I could feel changes in myself; big changes, a massive change of direction. Yet I'd seen and experienced very little compared to her. I could only marvel at the inner strength that had brought her this far.

But I did have to get her out of here.

I approached the warrant officer to sound him out on what might be done, but he was sceptical. "The city is closed-off," he said. "The Serbs won't let anyone through their checkpoints, and right now it would be suicide to even try. They'd shoot you down in a moment. We're bombing them, for fuck's sake."

"But she needs help," I said. "Surely you can see that?"

He nodded. "No question. But she's stuck here. We're all stuck here, until this thing pauses for breath. Do you think the French will let us get anywhere near the front line?"

I scurried to and fro, attending to my duties, spending time with Bella whenever I could. She managed to hold down some food, but I could see her nails had been bitten away and her fingers had been bleeding. Her room was strewn with empty cigarette packets and half-drunk bottles of water. She was surviving on her nerves, and her nerves were shot-away.

I determined to tackle the general about her, find out what the senior chain of command was prepared to do to help.

I waited until the major was busy on some important call, slipped past him, and then climbed into the general's outer office. The UN Head of Civil Affairs was sat to the left, an important man, a powerful man. He glanced at me disinterestedly, then buried his head in a pile of correspondence strewn across his desk. He looked tired and drawn, but then we all looked tired and drawn. It was that kind of a place, that kind of a time.

The general's office was off to the right, but its door was firmly closed. A couple of staff officers were engaged in urgent conversation, barring the way, though not intentionally. I made to slide past, intent on giving one knock then entering with or without permission. But one of the officers stopped me.

"He's on a call. What do you need?"

So I began to explain, and the man listened whilst his colleague busied himself at a nearby desk. There was no interruption so I continued, and the more I talked the more I wanted to talk; and the more I wanted to talk the faster my words flowed.

The officer perched his backside on the edge of his desk and his pale blue eyes stared into mine without blinking. I told him I'd never met anyone as brave as Lieutenant Harris, that she deserved to be taken care of because her spirit was broken and she needed to go home, that she'd given so much and her work was now done.

Then the officer asked if I had a plan. But I didn't have a plan because I was only a sergeant, and sergeants don't make plans, they *implement* plans and I was looking to him to give me a plan, or show me where I could get a plan. Because Lieutenant Harris needed a plan to get out of this place and into a hospital and away from the bombs and the guns and the blood and the death.

So he told me he'd give it some thought, told me to go and take care of her. And as I stumbled away he could surely see by my tears that I cared beyond reason, and that maybe I was as damaged as she.

The bombing ended abruptly, and we heard that the Serbs had been given a few days to lift the siege of Sarajevo or face a resumption of attacks. I strained for news of movement in and out of the city, but the place remained bottled-up in all directions and I despaired for Lieutenant Isabella Harris.

Then, quite unexpectedly, the warrant officer pulled me into a dark corner and said he'd been authorised by the general's office to facilitate an evacuation of Isabella by any means possible. He said he had a plan, but it was a risky one and it needed my help.

The following evening, we drove to the apartment block where Mirsad and Almira lived and knocked on their door.

"Hi there!" Almira sounded delighted, but puzzled. She glanced enquiringly at the warrant officer

"It's Bella," he said. "She's unwell."

Almira pushed the door open and we entered, then spent the next half hour telling her about Isabella's situation, explaining that we needed to get her out of here so she could be properly taken care of.

"Poor thing," said Almira. "Mirsad will be so sad to hear all this when he gets home. If there's anything we can do…"

"There is something you can do," said the warrant officer. "But we know it's a big ask."

"Anything at all…"

"We need to use the tunnel."

A beat.

"Tunnel? What tunnel?"

"The one under the airport, the one that the Bosnian Army has been using to resupply the city," he said. "It's the only way in. It's the only way out. Apart from going through the Sierras, and they're closed tight."

"I don't think…"

"Come on Almira," I said. "It's an open secret. Your people dug it more than two years ago. Bella needs to go. You can help. She's your friend."

She shook her head.

"I'm begging you," I said. "She's not eating. Barely drinking. She's a wreck."

"I think you need to go."

She herded us towards the door, pushed it open and shoved us through. I turned, stopping her from closing it shut.

"She loved your parents, Almira. Are you sure you can't help?"

She looked at me with those wide, staring eyes. "I'll speak with Mirsad. We know where to find you."

Then the door was closed and we drove back to the Residency.

CHAPTER 23

Everything was packed. We didn't need much. I knew the warrant officer wouldn't follow us out of the city if we managed to break free. His duties lay back here. Mine were done.

So were Bella's... poor, broken-down Bella. There was nothing to be done for her, except keep her supplied with water, food and cigarettes. She sat cross-legged on her bunk, sometimes rocking back and forth, sometimes humming tunelessly to herself.

She always smiled at me when I came in, and occasionally held my hand. But when I tried to hug her or kiss her, she stiffened and pulled away. It was as if some kind of barrier had grown between her and the surrounding world. I figured it was a protective device of some kind, but the warrant officer said it was just shock and that it would wear off in time.

It was by no means certain how the unending drama of Bosnia-Herzegovina would play-out. It seemed like the Serbs had no intention of giving-in to the demands of the UN, NATO or anyone else. It could only be a matter of time before the bombs started falling again.

Then suddenly the warrant officer was all energy and business. "It's on," he said. "This evening. Last light."

"The tunnel?"

"Be ready."

So in the fading light of day we loaded Lieutenant Harris into the familiar Land Rover and departed the Residency. I didn't look back. I hoped I'd never see the place again.

We met with Mirsad close to the Bosnian Presidency. He was dressed in a military uniform, but I was quite sure he wasn't part of the military. We ditched the Land Rover and crowded into a battered old saloon car. Isabella gave him a watery smile, but said nothing.

"You have the money?"

"Yes," said the warrant officer.

"Good."

"Are you coming through?" I asked.

"No, just you and Bella. It's the best I could do." He sounded nervous.

We drove towards the airport using a route I was unfamiliar with. The light was fading fast, but I could see horrendous war damage all around. Shadowy figures peered out from the ruins, heavily armed, keenly alert. The looming bulk of the airport terminal was away to our right. I could see dim lights being displayed by soldiers manning the terminal's checkpoint. But we bypassed them, snuck through on their flank, heading to the furthest extremes of the built-up area.

The vehicle stopped.

"Now, we walk," said Mirsad.

I had Isabella firmly by her arm. Mirsad walked slightly ahead of us, the warrant officer behind. There were low voices, the sound of weapons being handled. Then raised voices, and a sharp reprimand or something similar from our guide. Then on again, with Bosnian soldiers to our left and right. A short burst of tracer flew high overhead, loosed off from the end of the airfield. Then the crump of a mortar round uncomfortably close. We went to ground, waiting for things to settle. Isabella was breathing fast, squirming in my grip. I kept her firmly under control. Then up again, and on again; closer to a last line of buildings and to the airfield.

We brought up against the side of a heavily sandbagged house and were quickly shepherded inside through a series of heavy drapes. Several Bosnian soldiers were lounging around, smoking and drinking coffee. They looked at us aggressively. Some of them stood and groped for their weapons. But Mirsad was all words and orders and they slumped back sullenly. I realised that without authority and without explanation, they would have killed us just for being there.

"We go from here to the tunnel entrance," said Mirsad. "Pay half your fee when they ask. Do what they say. Pay half again at the other end. There will be a woman, she will tell you what to do. There will be a car, and a driver. He does not need money, he speaks English. He will take you to the bottom of Igman. From there you walk, the track is clear. Don't lose your way, there are mines. You will be across by first light. On the plateau, you will see British soldiers."

"They're expecting you," said the warrant officer. "Royal Artillery. They should have transport."

The soldiers were stirring.

"When we move, we move fast," said Mirsad. "The Serbs often shell. They know about the tunnel, but have never found the range."

I began to thank him, but he told me to keep quiet, that maybe we'd meet again one day when all this was over. And he told me to take care of Bella because she was a good friend and a good woman. Then we were out into the night with soldiers ahead of us and soldiers behind us, angling towards another house with darkness all around.

We were processed quickly at the entrance to the tunnel. Mirsad motioned me forward and I pressed a wad of cash into the hands of a man I could barely see. There was a steady stream of men spewing from the tunnel entrance, men carrying boxes and bags and burdens of all shapes and sizes. They were curving away into the dark, purposeful and determined, breathless and tired. Everything was fast and organized. Nobody lingered in this deadly place.

The stream of activity thinned, and then I was conscious of people pressing towards us from behind.

"It's time," said Mirsad.

The warrant officer was at my side. "Good luck," he said. "Get in touch with our people in Croatia. Take Bella there. Let us know you're OK."

I wanted to say something, but I had no words. We shook hands. I would never forget.

"Now, go." Mirsad clapped me on the shoulder. "Take care of her. This is all that matters."

Then they were gone, and I held the lieutenant's tiny hand firmly in mine as we descended a short flight of uneven steps into the ink-black mouth of Muslim Sarajevo's only link to the outside world.

Our first stumbling steps were uncertain and slow. I was conscious there were only a few men ahead of us, but I was certain there were many pressing from behind. Then the tunnel curved very slightly. Far ahead there was the dull glimmer of overhead lighting, just a few strip bulbs, dim and blue.

I banged my head on something solid and metallic. Someone behind us snapped on a flashlight. Then I could see that the tunnel was much narrower than I'd thought it would be, and lower too. It was lined to left and right with a mix of rough horizontal planks and sheets of rusted steel that seemed to have been cut from the sides of shipping containers. These were braced back vertically by logs of various thickness, which in turn were shoring a similar arrangement overhead. There was more planking underfoot, uneven and rough. Attached to this was a crude rail track. From the noise ahead, I guessed that some form of rolling stock was being pushed or driven to the far end.

We picked up the pace and the height of the tunnel reduced, forcing us to bend low. Our small backpacks kept catching on the roof. Someone behind us was cursing, probably telling us to get a move on. The air was thick and heavy, dust-laden and rancid. I noticed a small bore pipe, and from the smell of diesel I expected this was carrying fuel into the city.

Isabella was stumbling along behind me as we struggled to keep up with the small group of soldiers ahead. She said nothing, but I clutched her hand to keep her close as the tunnel dipped, taking us directly under the airport's runway.

Sweat began to run freely down my face, stinging my eyes, dripping from my chin. We followed the circle of light ahead. We passed the flickering bulbs, careful not to bang them with our heads or dislodge them with our packs. The tunnel reached its lowest point and there was water underfoot. Just a couple of inches, enough to make me wonder if they'd have a real problem with flooding when the weather became grim.

The men ahead were pressing on and the men behind were pushing hard. So I panted and sweated, and the muscles of my back twisted into a solid knot of pain; and Isabella's hand was slippery and thin and my stumbling feet struggled to maintain the pace as the tunnel climbed towards its exit.

The woman was waiting, stood at the top of the roughly hewn stairs. I could see by the light of the moon that she was traditionally dressed, a headscarf knotted under her chin, a full and flowing peasant's dress pinned tight around her waist. She handed us each a plastic cup filled with cool water, muttered *a salaam a'laikum,* then smiled a pale, toothy grin and pulled us to one side.

"Money?"

I handed her the remaining cash. She didn't check it.

"Follow men, quick. See someone."

There was no time for questions. Bullets were cracking overhead and close-by.

We were closer to the Serb lines here. I could see that the building was splattered with strike marks and shrapnel holes. The Serbs must be strafing this area for all they were worth if they knew about the tunnel, which of course they did, because there had been press articles about it and the Serbs themselves had often cited its existence as a breach of the ceasefire conditions. But then the ceasefire was over, so it was all a bit academic now.

The lieutenant was already following-on with the soldiers, so I caught up with her and took her hand once again. We tripped and slid across a heavily rutted road and along the wall of a house opposite, jostling with soldiers and other men dressed in the rough clothes of an armed militia.

There were shell scrapes and craters underfoot, dirt and dust and the faecal smell of excrement rising with the dust. Then we were into a shallow ditch and the men around us were bent double, stumbling and falling, anxious to put distance between themselves and the tunnel. Tracer fire was cracking across the surrounding fields. I realised that we were traversing along the frontline itself, headed towards the foot of Mount Igman.

Two loud explosions ahead had everyone eating dirt. I threw myself on top of Isabella as shrapnel hissed overhead. Then we were up again and running, and my chest hurt with the exertion and Bella was grunting with the effort. I could see her eyes wide and bright and I was hoping she could hold it in, stay with me, dig deep.

The trench carried us into the suburb of Butmir. As we reach its end a man pulled the pair of us away from the crowd and led us to a small, battered car.

"In."

We crowded onto the back seat.

"Stay down."

The vehicle lurched forward, no lights, its fan belt squealing, exhaust spluttering. In a short while we were negotiating a small bridge over a thin river and then lurching our way along a narrow road through another dark town.

I tried asking the driver what we could expect next, but he told me to keep quiet and to stay down. So I hugged the lieutenant and I wondered if all this was the right thing to be doing because she seemed to be taking things with remarkable calm and maybe she would have been fine back at the Residency if we'd just waited it out. But we were here, and it was pointless thinking like that because there was no way back, though God knew what lay ahead.

"Hrasnica," said the driver. I knew this to be good news because the town lay at the very foot of Mount Igman. "Wait here." He disappeared into the night.

"Are you OK, Bella?" I asked.

"I'm fine," she said, and she did sound fine.

"Ready to walk?"

"Yes. Can I have a cigarette?"

"Not yet."

"Please."

"We'll ask the driver if it's OK."

She tried to get out of the car, but I held her firm and she didn't struggle.

The driver returned with another man. "Come."

They led us on foot along a side street. The mountain loomed over us, dark and foreboding.

Isabella tugged on the driver's sleeve. "Can I have a cigarette?"

"No."

She said something in Serbo-Croat. His companion responded sharply, turned, and shined a flashlight directly into her eyes. There was a sharp intake of breath, and then heated words between the two men. Isabella grabbed me, and I could feel that she was shaking.

"What's the problem?"

"He knows me."

"The driver?"

"The other one."

The two men were still arguing, and we were going nowhere. Then Bella had a gun in her hand, and I hadn't known that she was carrying a gun. I pushed her arm down.

"If he does anything, I'll kill him," she hissed. I did not doubt for a moment that she would.

"How does he know you?"

"He was at the guard post when we evacuated the old man and the woman. Last year."

It took me a moment to remember, but then I did. "He thinks you're a whore?"

"He thinks I'm a spy."

Oh dear, sweet Isabella. So does everyone else, I thought. But I un-holstered my pistol and kept it by my side, ready for instant use if needed.

"Can we go?" I asked the driver.

"Yes."

We continued, but the lieutenant stayed a pace behind me. I could see our new companion looking over his shoulder, but the driver shoved him in the back and we continued through the streets until we reached the edge of town.

"This man will take you from here," said the driver. "He has no English, but your woman can understand."

"Thank you."

"It is nothing. He will show you a path. When it reaches the Igman road, turn left and keep going up. If the French come in their armoured vehicles, hide. They will take you back to the city. You people are on the reverse slope, with their big guns. Goodbye." And he was gone.

We followed along behind our new guide. The pace was steady, but the sweat flowed freely and I was cursing the fact that we hadn't brought any water. I could see that the lieutenant still had her gun in her free hand, but I'd packed mine away because the guide was pressing on and in any case we were completely in his hands. If he wanted to do something stupid, I was quite sure that Bella would shoot him down in an instant anyhow.

Scattered clouds overhead accelerated across a starlit sky as we gained altitude. One moment we were bathed in pale light, the next we were stumbling our way through the dark, twisting our ankles and tripping on rocks. We didn't dare to show any light. Although we were moving deeper and deeper into the Demilitarised Zone, we would have been fools to think that this was by any measure a safe place.

"Follow."

We stopped at the edge of a tarmac road and our guide was pointing uphill. From here we were on our own, and I knew it was a straight shot to the Igman plateau. I offered my hand but the man refused to take it. He brushed past us, heading back the way we'd come. The lieutenant raised her gun, aiming it at his back, but I held onto her arm and then he was gone.

"Are you OK?" I asked.

"He's a brute."

"He helped us."

"You don't know what he said to me."

"What did he say?"

"You don't want to know."

I didn't push it. She had her reasons for keeping it tight. She had her reasons for keeping so many things tight.

We continued towards the top of the mountain. I felt uncomfortable at following the road because ambushes are most usually laid on linear features, but we didn't have much of a choice. The land to left and right was probably sown with mines, and in any case we had neither water nor food. We needed to make contact with the British position.

The air was cooler up here and we plodded on through the night. Once in a while we could see the city spread out below us. Even at this late hour the occasional burst of tracer flickered across the front line from the Grbavica suburb, just enough to keep people on their toes, just enough to keep children awake.

We passed a small group of burned-out houses and then a turning that led towards the abandoned ski fields with their wrecked lift system, the road upon which poor old Bagley and

I had taken with the French in their freezing cold armoured personnel carrier all that time ago.

As we crested the extended plateau that marked the top of the Mount Igman massif we could see the looming bulk of Bjelasnica to our west. I wondered how the Muslims had managed to maintain their supply route across that huge mountain. I worried about the Serb offensive I knew had been advancing through this terrain. I had no idea where the British were, or how we could make contact with them.

Then a series of massive explosions slammed through the night air. The mountainside lit up with bright flashes and we sprawled on the ground. I knew in a moment that we would have no problem at all in finding the British artillery position, because there they were in all their percussive glory, firing off a half dozen salvos as NATO and the UN recommenced their bombardment of Serb positions in and around the city. A blind or a deaf man could have figured where they were.

I turned towards Isabella to make sure that she was OK, but she was on all fours, scrambling away down the hill and I could tell that she was panicking. I ran after her and try to get her to stop, but she had energy and strength and I knew straight away that it would be impossible to have her go anywhere near the artillery line whilst the guns were still firing.

Then ahead of us I could see tracer rounds arcing up the hill, and then there were tracer rounds coming down the hill over our heads and dangerously close; so I wondered if we were caught in a firefight or been mistaken for the enemy. I forced Isabella to stop and we lay together on the ground, shaking and shivering as the drama ran its course. Then the artillery checked fire and everything fell silent once more.

It was clearly too risky to approach the artillery line, and in any case I didn't think I could persuade Bella to go that way. I pulled out my map, and with Isabella lying on the ground close beside me and my combat smock pulled over our heads, I made a quick appreciation of the ground. I decided that the safest thing to do would be to flank around the British position, and then continue over the top of the mountain and down the other side to the main road towards the town of Kilseljak.

The wind was whipping around us as I explained this to Isabella. She nodded and agreed, but I really couldn't tell if she understood what I meant. So I took her by the hand and we stood and began walking uphill, slowly and carefully, protected by the sounds of the wind and by dust being kicked up like a cloud all around.

My knee was beginning to hurt like hell, but there really was no choice. We had to clear out from this area. It was stupid to come here, stupid to think that we could link up with the British. What on Earth had I been thinking?

But then it wasn't my plan, it was the warrant officer's plan; and the plan had been approved by the general. But then maybe the general hadn't known about the plan, and the plan had been kept secret from him because it was a stupid plan and a dangerous plan. And the Observers were a law unto themselves in any case.

But here we were, and the mountain was high but the weather was warm. Once in a while we took to the ground when the guns let rip and the clouds reflected their muzzle flashes. The air became cooler as we climbed. Then we found a track that ran away around the side of the mountain with forest on either side, so we followed the track and I thought to hell with the possibility of an ambush. Isabella stuck with it, hugging herself for warmth, head bent low against the wind, following without question.

The night wore on and the guns were far below us, but silent now. All I could hear was the wind howling around us. I knew we had to keep moving.

I glanced over my shoulder, but she wasn't there. I ran back down the track, panic rising in my breast. But there she was, sat on a log at the side of the track, curled into a tight ball and shivering. I sat beside her and hugged her, trying to share a little warmth.

"We have to keep going, Bella," I said. "We'll be across the top soon and then it will be easier."

She nodded and looked up at me.

"We are having a grand adventure, aren't we?" she asked.

I told that of course we were, this was all part of some heroic story that we could recount to our grandchildren when we were old and fat and grey. But that first we had to walk across this wretched mountain and find the road on the other side before it got light. So she stood and we plodded on once more, forever upwards, into the thinner air.

I got a little ahead of her again, and then without warning there were shots from behind so I span around and there was Isabella firing back down the track. I pulled out my gun and ran back to her, and she screamed that it was the man who'd recognised her, that he'd tried to grab her but she'd shot him. He had disappeared and I didn't know if he was hit, or if it really was that man, or even if there was a man at all.

So I pulled her onwards and kept my gun in my hand and hoped that if it really had been someone he was dead and unable to come after us again, or call for help, or tell anyone ahead that we were following the track.

The first light of day brought form and substance to the track and the trees, and we were enveloped in mist, which was probably a blessing. The ground was falling away beneath our feet as we stumbled along. I could feel blisters on my heels and my knee was swollen and angry. The forest was thicker, encroaching from either side, but the air was warmer and I began to feel that maybe we'd be fine.

We found a small stream by the side of the track and drank its fresh, cold water, and nothing had ever tasted so good. Soon the trees began to thin, and then we were crossing a field and climbing a fence, and then there was the road.

I knew from the state of my feet and the aching in my belly and the distance on the map that we wouldn't be walking all the way to Kiseljak. So we took up a position by the side of the road to wait for a vehicle, set back a little and hidden from view. The morning air began to warm. I looked at Lieutenant Isabella Harris.

She was curled into a little ball on the ground, fast asleep.

CHAPTER 24

"You came from where?"

The officer sounded incredulous, and I couldn't blame him. It was not every day that British soldiers who'd been seconded to UNPROFOR walked clear across the Demilitarised Zone with its landmines, its Bosnian resupply route, its war-fighting and, latterly, its concentrations of United Nations artillery. He clearly hadn't received any word from the Residency about us, and I could see he was finding my story very hard to swallow.

I didn't try explaining any further. He could check with the general's headquarters. I waited outside his office for what seemed to be an eternity until a young corporal came out and told me that I was to wait for the next convoy down to the coast and join the Observers' rear echelon and await further orders. I told him that I couldn't leave the lieutenant, that she was my responsibility and that I had to stay with her.

So he checked with the officer and came back out to tell me that I had no choice because I was not a casualty and I was not a medic and that they had no authority to transport passengers or casual escorts with battle casualties, which Lieutenant Harris clearly was; and in any case didn't I know that Lieutenant Harris was suffering post-traumatic stress and had lost a significant amount of body weight, and that she didn't need anyone creating any more stress for her?

So I asked him to tell the captain that of course I knew all that, but that the lieutenant was my partner and that I loved her.

Then the captain came out and looked at me oddly and told me that Lieutenant Harris would be taken care of, and that my orders were to proceed to the city of Split in Croatia and report to the Observer's rear echelon, and that there would be no more arguing about that.

I stormed away and stomped around the headquarters, scowling at anyone in a uniform and wishing that I wasn't in a uniform and trying to figure what to do.

I attempted to see Isabella in the small medical centre situated at the rear of the headquarters, but she wasn't there because they'd put her into isolation inside the main building as if she had a contagious disease or something. Or maybe they believed she *did* have a contagious disease, because wasn't post-traumatic stress just another expression for shell shock or battle fatigue, and didn't those things have a military connotation that suggested *cowardice in the face of the enemy*?

The more I thought along those lines the more I thought I needed to do something outlandish and outrageous. In due course I hatched a plan to kidnap the lieutenant and spirit her away towards where she really needed to go.

It wasn't hard to do. In fact, my plan, when it came to me, was startlingly simple. All it would take was a diesel-soaked rag and the theft of a vehicle.

I scouted the parking area, selected a chariot that still had its keys in the ignition, and then dipped a rag in its fuel tank. A few minutes later the entire headquarters was emptying of personnel as fire evacuation procedures stalled the business of the day, because there's nothing quite like a diesel-soaked rag on fire to generate a huge amount of smoke.

I watched the exodus intently. Sure enough there she was, dressed in some kind of tracksuit they'd given her in lieu of proper bedclothes, all willowy and wonderful, though as pale as death. I angled towards her, took her firmly by the arm and led her away from the confusion.

"What are you doing?"

"Shhhh. We're heading out."

"But my clothes…"

"Don't worry." I loaded her into the vehicle.

"Where are we going?" Her voice was slurred. They'd probably dosed her up with some kind of tranquiliser.

"Where we were told to go. Croatia."

The vehicle started first time and we rolled towards the exit. Smoke was billowing from the ground floor storage room where I'd placed the burning rag. Nobody challenged us or tried to stop us. Everyone was watching the fire drill run its course.

The fastest way to the Croatian coast was along the main road towards the shattered city of Mostar, but I knew this to be blocked off by the warring factions. The only alternative was to head deeper into central Bosnia and take a mountain road cut by the Royal Engineers that was called Route Triangle. I glanced at the lieutenant and could see that she was shivering, though whether from cold, fear or just anxiety I couldn't tell.

"There's a spare uniform in that bag," I said. "You should put it on."

She nodded, and before I could suggest otherwise had pulled off her tracksuit top. I was shocked at how thin she'd become, how her ribs were protruding like that of a cancer victim. She saw me watching and giggled.

"Put on the uniform," I said.

She pouted. "I don't have my identity card, or my passport."

"We'll figure it."

She put on the uniform and within minutes was asleep, slumped against the door.

I wondered if we'd be reported as deserters, but I didn't care. I was done with the Army and done with this country. All that mattered was to get Isabella out of there and down to the coast.

The Observers had said they would help. Bella needed help. She deserved help. Maybe I should have left her with the people at Kiseljak. Maybe I was getting this wrong. But if they wouldn't let me go with her, then she had to come with me.

I gunned the vehicle's engine, driving as fast as I could. Driving into the gloom of the late afternoon, across Bosnia-Herzegovina. Driving towards Route Triangle with its treacherous mountain road; driving towards any number of checkpoints guarded by rough men with their guns and their questions and their greedy eyes.

Driving away from bombs and bullets and the endless parade of death that had come to define the tragic city of Sarajevo.

CHAPTER 25

"You want to leave the Army?" It was more of a statement than a question.

"I do."

The Observer staff sergeant gave me a hard up-from-under look. "Because of this woman?"

"Yes."

He pushed his chair back from the table and placed his hands behind his head. He was an old soldier, at least that's the way he looked to me. Big without being fat, short haired without being bald. He had a thick black moustache that was flecked with grey, and pale blue eyes that were deeply set under bushy eyebrows. His forearms must have been as thick as my thighs, and he had tattoos that suggested no prisoners were likely to be taken.

"So you want to leave the Army for love?"

"I want to leave the Army to take care of Isabella," I said.

"We're on operations, son. Nobody leaves the Army when they're on operations."

"It's not our war."

He grunted. "It rarely is."

"She resigned her Commission. She's a civilian now. She won't go home, you know that."

The staff sergeant leaned forward and looked again at a signal on his desk. "Says here you've been given a month of leave, then you're posted back to your unit in the UK."

"If I have a month of leave, I'm staying here."

"Fair enough. What will you do if the Army won't let you go?"

I shrugged. "I don't know."

He rocked back on his chair again. "Well you should figure it out."

"I won't leave her."

"No, I don't think you will." He stood and walked me to the door. "Off you go then. Enjoy your leave. We'll let your unit know." He caught my arm as I passed him. "I'll speak with our people. Let you know if anything can be done."

"Thank you."

"Take good care of her. Brave lass. That's what I've been told."

Isabella was sat on the terrace when I got to the apartment. We'd rented a small place overlooking the harbour at Trogir, a few miles north of the city. I was meant to be staying with the British Forces in the old Yugoslav military barracks back in Split where the staff sergeant was based, but it was all horribly regimental. And in any case Isabella needed me, and I needed Isabella, so to hell with all that.

"Hello darling," she said, shooting me the sad, wan smile that had become so familiar and that broke my heart every time it was deployed. "I missed you."

I joined her on the terrace and was pleased that she seemed to have more colour in her face and that she didn't smell of smoke when I kissed her cheek, and that her hands no longer shook as if she had Parkinson's Disease or early onset Alzheimer's.

"I missed you too," I said.

"What did they tell you?"

"That I have to report to my unit in the UK when my leave is over."

"That's too bad," she said.

"It's more than bad, it's infuriating."

"You shouldn't worry."

"I won't go back."

"Just resign your Commission darling. I did."

"I'm not an officer, Bella. I can't do that."

"Then go absent. We'll run away. It will be such fun…"

I laughed, and it was good to laugh. We hadn't done enough laughing since arriving here after that goddam awful journey from the heart of Bosnia and across Route Triangle with its treacherous road surface and its hairpin bends and the thieves and the militia hiding in its forests just waiting for a chance to rob or even to kill you. Then on, past the guards at the checkpoints with their questions and their distrust, and the men on the border who were curiously sympathetic to a lone soldier and a sleeping woman with no papers. Men who were happy to accept the last of our money as the price for passage into Croatia.

I had tried to get her to a doctor, of course, and tried to have a doctor visit her in the apartment. But she had refused or they had refused, and in the end I'd had to accept that this is how things were and to take each day as a new challenge and a new opportunity. To love her and to hold her, or watch her quietly from a distance as she battled the demons that tormented her soul.

"I thought we might take a walk this afternoon," I said. "Watch the fishermen land their catch, buy something for dinner."

"That would be nice."

"It will be good to get out for a while."

"I like it in here," she said.

"It is very lovely."

"So are you."

I kissed her head and she held onto my wrist. "You will stay with me won't you?" she asked.

"Of course I will."

"You won't take me to the doctor will you?"

"Not unless you want to go."

"Shall we go to see the fishermen this afternoon?"

"That sounds like a lovely idea," I said, pretending it was her idea.

So with the sun westering across the Adriatic we walked hand in hand down to the tiny harbour and watched old men with leathered skin offloading boxes of fish packed in ice onto the quayside from their brightly coloured skiffs; and young men on the quay sorting through each box and separating the catch species by species and size by size, shouting prices to local women who haggled over the price, paid with cash and then scurried away, anxious to get their fish into the fridge or freezer or the dinner plate at home.

Then Bella joined in and argued the price of one big fat silver fish that I didn't even recognise, and a young man smiled, and an old fisherman, with particularly dark skin and deep wrinkles on his face, laughed and said something to the boy, who laughed and said something to Bella; who laughed in turn and looked at me and they all laughed, and I knew that the joke was at my expense.

So I laughed too, and we paid for the beautiful fat fish at a knockdown price and took it back to the apartment. I filleted the fish and Bella grilled it on the terrace using a charcoal barbecue of vintage years and questionable hygiene.

Then we ate the fish and drank cold white wine, and as the last rays of the sun melted across the far horizon we made slow, tender love on a sheepskin rug spread on the tiled floor of our small home, and I knew that I would stay with this beautiful, haunted woman until the end.

CHAPTER 26

I had been so worried about coming to this place but now I could see it was after all what Isabella needed.

Nothing much of war had touched the area around the island town of Trogir. This was a relief because I'd had enough of war with its tears and its grief, its calamities and atrocities, its pain and its death. I shielded Bella from the news of Bosnia because I knew it distressed her, and we walked the streets of this fine old place with its cafes and churches and shops.

There were people here in uniform, of course. I could feel Isabella's grip on my hand tighten whenever we passed members of the military, and then it seemed I was leading a young child who was uncertain of herself, frightened to be alone, anxious to go home. Usually I could persuade her that everything would be fine, and we would continue to walk the narrow streets.

But sometimes her anxiety raised tears or hysteria, and then I knew she would not settle until we were back in the apartment with its door closed and bolted. Then she would cling to me and I would kiss her and she would calm down and apologise and say that next time she'd be perfectly OK and that I mustn't worry about her because she was getting better every day and that very soon not even those bastards in Bosnia would be able to scare her anymore.

Every day I hoped to hear something from the staff sergeant down in Split, but everything remained quiet. As the days passed, I could feel the inexorable pull of the Army drawing me back. But every time Isabella asked if it was time for me to go, I reassured her that I would never leave, and she told me I had to leave if it was my duty to leave. So I said that my duty was to her alone and that I no longer cared about the Army.

I awoke early one morning and she was gone. I jumped out of bed, called her name and pulled on my clothes, terrified that I wouldn't find her. But there she was, sat on the sea wall near the fish dock, smoking a cigarette and shivering in the grey light of dawn.

"What are you doing here?" I asked, sitting beside her.

"Couldn't sleep," she said. A gentle breeze was playing around her hair, making it billow and catch in the corner of her mouth. She stubbed her cigarette and flicked it into the sea.

"Bad dreams?"

"No."

"What then?"

"I don't know." Her grey eyes stared out over the grey water and she hugged her knees. "Just thinking."

"You think too much."

"I do, don't I?"

"May I sit with you?"

"That would be nice."

So I shuffled close beside her and drew her in. I could feel that she was cold. "Can I take you to see a doctor?" I asked.

"No."

"It might help."

"Nobody can help."

Her head was resting on my shoulder. I knew it was pointless pursuing the issue. We'd had this conversation dozens of times. She wouldn't change her mind.

"You're shivering," she said.

"It's cold. You're cold."

"That's true. Shall we walk?"

The waterfront was quiet and the sound of our footsteps echoed off the ancient buildings that lined the quay. A couple of small boats were moored to the sea wall, rolling gently against their fenders and pulling at their lines.

"Wouldn't it be lovely to go sailing?" asked Isabella.

I said that would be grand but I doubted there would be any boats for hire. And that in any case, there were probably restrictions on the movement of boats along the coast because there was still a lot of tension throughout the Balkans and the war wasn't over yet.

Then I wished I hadn't mentioned the war because I could feel her hand tighten and I wondered if we were about to head back to the apartment, but she held it down and we continued to walk as the sun rose above the horizon and spread its glorious light across the entire harbour.

The first café had opened its shutters and the proprietor was placing his tables and chairs on the patio. So we stopped and ordered coffee and pastries that he served without a smile. We sat and ate the pastries and sipped our coffee in wonderful silence as the sun warmed our shoulders and the town awoke around us.

"It would be nice, wouldn't it?" asked Isabella presently.

"What would be nice?"

"To take a boat somewhere."

"You're serious?"

She smiled at me and pouted her lower lip. "Of course I am."

"Could be expensive."

"I have money."

"Might not be possible."

A bigger pout. "You'll make it work."

"I suppose I could try," I said.

Then she sat on my lap with her arms around my neck, and of course I knew I had to try.

There was a message waiting from the staff sergeant when we got back home. He wanted to see me, so I took a shower and shaved and put on my uniform, and then rode a taxi to the barracks to hear his news.

"Your leg hurting?" he asked as soon as I entered his office.

"No more than usual."

"I'm sure you said it was giving you hell last time I saw you."

"I don't think so."

"Better sit down," he said.

"Why's that?"

"Because your leg's hurting you so much."

I didn't get it, but sat anyway.

The staff sergeant had something of a self-satisfied smirk on his face. "You said you wanted to leave the Army, right?" he asked.

"That's what I said."

"You still want to leave?"

"You know I do."

He slid a bunch of papers across his desk. "All you need to do is sign."

I picked up the documents and shuffled through them. "These are my discharge papers?" My voice sounded incredulous, even to me.

"Not exactly, son. You'll need to see an Army doctor so he can make recommendations to the Medical Review Board. But all you'll need to do is squeal every time he twists your knee."

"Medical discharge?"

"It was a bad injury. No surprise it broke down on you, what with going back on operations and all that."

"How did you swing it?"

"There's always a way in our outfit. Nobody has to stay if they don't want to."

"Your outfit?"

"You know what I mean."

I didn't know what he meant, not really. The Observers had always been a mystery to me. I was just attached to them. I had no idea what they really were, and I didn't actually care. I had my ticket to leave. The rest would be just a formality.

"Where do I sign?"

He showed me, and it was done.

"It will take a couple of weeks," he said. "I'll let you know."

"Thank you," I said.

"No problem. Now bugger off."

Back at the apartment Isabella was cooking pasta. I'd picked up some flowers and a fine bottle of rosé, which I set on the kitchen table.

"How did it go?" she asked.

"I resigned my Commission," I said. "I'll be out in a fortnight."

She squealed, threw her arms around my neck and kissed me full on the lips. "See?" she said. "I told you that was the thing to do!"

CHAPTER 27

One of the fishermen down at the dock who had decent English explained to me that many boat owners took their yachts across to Italy before hostilities broke out, but others had simply moved them to quiet islands offshore, out of range of the artillery. His brother had a sailing yacht, he said, moored at Korcula away to the south. He could arrange for it to be brought to Trogir if I could pay the price.

He reassured me she was in fine condition, and that if I gave him one hundred euros or one hundred American dollars or one hundred English pounds, he would shake my hand and I would see her within a week.

So I said *of course I will* and counted out the equivalent of one hundred euros in local currency because that seemed like a fair deposit to me. We shook, and his skin was rough and his hand was strong, but I felt he was a man to be trusted.

I kept the news from Isabella because I wanted it to be a surprise, and then of course when one week became two weeks I wondered why I was the one who was surprised. But the fisherman was apologetic and offered me a refund on the deposit, so I told him I was sure he'd deliver on his promise and hoped that the boat would arrive ahead of the colder weather because it would be nice to take a slow voyage whilst the days were still bright and the sea was not rough.

My discharge papers came through before the yacht was delivered. When I handed in my identity card and my uniform to the staff sergeant I felt a little sad because I'd always thought the Army would provide me a full career and that sooner or later maybe I'd have received the Queen's Commission and become an officer.

But that was before I'd seen the effects of this thing called *war*. It was during my age of innocence, when the call to duty had seemed like a promise of glorious adventure in faraway lands. The Balkans had dislocated the myth and exposed the reality. It had laid bare the harsh, metallic truth: war is a brutal and disgusting thing.

I was glad to be leaving all of that that behind.

We celebrated my new-found freedom with many glasses of wine and a delicious moussaka that Isabella cooked in our chipped enamel oven, and for the first time in forever I felt hopeful for the future. I made a conscious decision to studiously ignore the ongoing situation in Bosnia-Herzegovina and concentrate all my attention on caring for Isabella Harris. I snuggled-up to her in bed and fell into a dreamless sleep that lasted well into mid-morning the following day.

The boat arrived, and I could see at once that she wasn't exactly ready for sea. She was a decent size, about thirty feet overall from stern to bow, and solid too. She had a conventional sloop rig that appeared quite capable of carrying an adequate suit of sails, but the caulking in her deck was loose and she had a couple of split planks in her clinker-build hull. I asked the fisherman if he would lend me some tools, and he agreed to see what he could do.

I spent the next couple of weeks sneaking away for a few hours a day to work on the yacht, and the fisherman supplied me with cotton caulking, sealant and assorted tools of varying utility. Repairing the deck was relatively straightforward, though when the job was finished I was under no illusions that it would last very long. The damaged hull planking was more problematic, but my new friend produced some copper sheeting, tacks and a silicone mastic that afforded a temporary repair good enough to last a season. I patched over the split planks, and then set about cleaning the yacht's interior and sorting through her rigging.

"Your hands are rough," said Isabella one day. "What have you been doing?"

"Helping out down at the dock," I replied. "I'm hoping they'll start paying me."

She laughed. "We do need an income," she said. "Maybe you'll become a fisherman?"

"Maybe I will. They seem like good people."

"You cannot trust them though," she said.

"Why not?"

"You can't trust any of them."

"Why not, Bella? They're good, working class men."

"You can't trust anyone in this country."

"Then let's go home, back to England," I said.

"This is my home." She went into the bedroom and slammed the door.

She'd been so good, but it was always there, just under the surface. I needed to get her away from here for a while, give her an alternative focus.

I continued to work on the boat, and then it was done. The fisherman had been helping me these past couple of days, careening the boat and giving her entire hull a fresh coat of bright yellow paint. We refloated her on the full tide, and tied her off at the town quay in Trogir.

"Your lady will love her," said the fisherman.

"That's what I'm hoping."

"You can buy the boat for five thousand euros," he said.

"I don't have that kind of money."

"Four thousand, then."

"It would be a bargain. But we agreed two hundred and fifty for a month's charter. That will have to do."

"Three thousand?" he asked.

"Two thousand five hundred?"

"You are a hard man." He offered his hand.

So I bought the yacht from the fisherman and his brother for two and a half thousand euros and now I really did need to begin looking for a job. But not just yet, because the daytime weather was still warm and Isabella wanted to go for a cruise along the coast. After that, we could start thinking about what we needed to do for the future.

The following morning, I took Bella for an early breakfast in the café with the humourless proprietor. She was calm and fey and lovely. The morning sun was shining on her hair and I was bursting to reveal my surprise. She could tell I was excited about something, and she asked me what it was.

"Oh, nothing much," I said, drinking the last of my coffee and smiling at her across the table.

"Tell me," she said.

"Soon."

"Now! I demand it. I'm an officer, you know."

"Not anymore," I said.

"That's true."

"Come on, then. I'll show you."

We walked across the road and stood at the edge of the quay.

"There you are," I said.

"What?" She was looking out across the water to the houses on the far side of the fairway.

"There."

"Where?"

"Under your toes."

She looked down. "The boat?"

"It's ours."

"Really?"

"Absolutely. That's what I've been working on, with the fisherman."

She jumped onboard and the boat bobbed in the water and pulled on its lines and rolled against the quayside as she made her way aft to the cockpit.

"Come on!" she said.

So I joined her and we explored together, bumping our heads on the low deckhead and stubbing our toes on the uneven cabin sole, and testing out the thin bunk cushions with our skinny backsides. We laughed and smiled and felt that wonderful sense of new-found freedom that comes with the certain knowledge that when you cast off the lines of a boat the sea can take you anywhere you choose, provided you have the time and the substance and the courage to leave the harbour behind.

"This is really ours to keep?" asked Bella. "Forever?"

"If she lasts that long," I replied.

So she hugged me and kissed me and we sat in the cockpit making plans for our first voyage together. And Bella had love in her eyes and a breathless energy in her voice, and I began to think that this would have been money well spent.

"What's her name?" she asked.

Strange, that hadn't occurred to me. The papers didn't stipulate a name, just a registration number. There was no name on the bow or on the transom.

"I don't know," I said. "We should think of one."

"We can have a naming ceremony," said Bella. "And your friend the fisherman can bless her."

"That would be nice."

"It would."

So we discussed names and agreed that we didn't want the yacht to have one of those trite and silly names; nor did we want some grand and heroic name, or the name of a god or some mythological sea creature. Then after three solid hours of suggestions and counter-suggestions, of making lists and scoring them out, of laughing and arguing and agreeing to disagree, we came to the conclusion that the naming of a yacht is harder than the naming of a child, and that we should simply leave it to the fisherman to decide. Because he must have owned many boats over the years and would be much better at this kind of thing than we could ever hope to be.

I started the yacht's tiny engine and we slipped the lines and motored her to a swinging mooring a few hundred yards offshore. Then we rowed back ashore in a small inflatable dinghy that served as the yacht's tender and ate lunch in our usual café before heading home arm-in-arm, excited for the future and anxious to take our maiden voyage before the winter set-in.

Three days later, we brought the yacht back to the town quay just before high tide and kedged her bows-in to the wall. The fisherman was waiting for us. He had a small bible and a bottle of cheap white wine, and was wearing his Sunday best.

We clambered ashore and stood in the watery sunshine whilst the fisherman said a prayer, crossed himself a few times, pressed the bottle against his bible, and then tipped a decent measure of wine over the yacht's bow.

"I name this boat the *Balkan Princess*," he said. "Because I know that both she and Isabella are princesses. May she keep you warm and safe in troubled waters."

He drank a good slug of wine straight from the bottle, and then invited each of us to repeat the process. "One measure for the boat," he said, "and three for the crew."

"Three for the crew?" I asked.

"I will come on your maiden voyage," he declared, solemnly.

Then we discovered that our maiden voyage consisted of a short trip to his fishing boat, which was at anchor nearby. He clambered onboard and waved goodbye as we bore away towards our mooring buoy.

"He's so sweet," said Isabella.

"He is."

"So are you."

"That's sweet."

"I do love you," she said.

"I know."

"No matter what happens, I shall always love you."

"What will happen?"

"Nothing."

"Nothing?"

"No, nothing at all," she said.

But she did sound a little sad.

CHAPTER 28

The following day we slipped our mooring and struck out northwest, hugging the coast, not yet confident enough to venture further offshore.

I'd managed to find some second-hand charts and could see that the islets and inlets that defined the Dalmatian Coast stretched northwest for a hundred and fifty miles or more. Our plan was to travel just a few days out and then head back, stopping wherever the fancy took us, drinking cheap wine and eating simple food.

We already had grander voyages planned for the spring, but for now all we needed was a shakedown cruise, enough to make sure our little craft was sound enough for more ambitious passages, enough time onboard to ensure this is really what we wanted to be doing.

We cleared the point and a steady wind set-in, fine on our starboard bow. So we raised the mainsail to its first reef and unfurled two thirds of the genoa, sufficient for the breeze, enough to get us sailing. I cut the engine and all was silent, save for a slatting of the sails and the sound of the sea.

"This is wonderful," declared Isabella, her hair blowing around her face. She looked radiant and alive, happier than I'd ever seen her. My heart lifted with the swell of the sea, so I snugged-up and had her helm the tiller under my guidance until she got the feel for how things were done.

Our little boat had a sweet motion that was neither racy nor sluggish. Her sails were grey and worn, but everything seemed well-found. We made steady progress to windward with the sea darkening to a deeper blue as the coast fell away and the sun climbed high overhead.

Presently Isabella seemed confident enough to be left alone on the helm, so I disappeared below and brewed hot coffee on the tiny gas cooker. I brought the coffee into the cockpit in plastic mugs with tight-fitting lids, then produced two slices of cake that I'd smuggled onboard hidden in a tin box. We resumed our position together on the helm and drank coffee and ate cake and kept each other warm as the day moved on and the coast wore away, and as gulls skimmed across the crests of breaking waves.

Late in the afternoon we tacked the yacht and closed with the coast to weather a dramatic headland with waves breaking across angry looking rocks close inshore. It was cooler now, and the sun was dipping towards the horizon as we started the engine, furled the genoa, dropped the main and motored into a secluded inlet where the chart suggested we'd find good holding ground for our anchor.

The chart proved to be correct, and with the last light of day chasing westwards across a darkening sky we pulled the cork on a bottle of crisp sauvignon that had been chilling beneath the cabin sole, and ate pasta stirred into a thick Bolognese sauce that had been warmed through on our tin-pot stove.

We had a lovely time on our tiny yacht the *Balkan Princess*; a time of peace and tranquillity, a time of carefree loving, a time of romance and delight. We continued northwards for another two days, learning how to sail our floating home to best effect. Learning how to live in this confined space, and learning that true intimacy recognised no boundaries. The sky above had no ceiling, the sea below held no fear, and in the careless way of young love we held and touched each other with an eager passion that cast all doubt aside.

In these days and in these moments, I knew that this woman had become, and would surely remain, the love of my life.

We returned southwards on a dead run with the main sheeted out and the genoa hauled across to the opposite side of the yacht with its sheet led through the end of a tightly braced spinnaker pole.

Our little ship rolled and yawed and we noticed a tendency to round-up, so we took in a reef on the main, and that balanced her to a point where she was almost sailing herself. But the motion of the yacht made us feel ill, and Isabella laughed at me when I threw-up over the side. But I had my revenge when she did the same not twenty minutes later, and I held on to her belt and thought we should be wearing lifejackets or lifelines or something. But then neither of us cared very much about any of that because there is no sensation at all that is quite so miserable as *mal de mer*.

Then we were under the lee of the land, with Trogir ahead of us and the sea calming down. We dropped all sail, started the engine and picked our way through the small fleet of crayfishers and longliners dotted around the bay before picking up our mooring.

Then we slept until the sound of rain beating on the deck woke us, and as we emerged from the warmth of our tiny cabin the first chill winds of winter were playing around the rigging and thick grey clouds were rolling down from the hills above the town.

CHAPTER 29

Isabella's nightmares returned.

I knew this to be so, because she was awaking every morning long before dawn. One morning I found her sitting on the terrace staring out across the grey water with a cigarette in her hand and barely enough clothes around her slender frame to ward off hypothermia.

"Come inside," I said.

"I don't want to come inside."

"You're freezing."

"Am I?"

"You know you are."

"I don't care," she said.

"Well, I do. Please come inside, Bella." I put an arm around her shoulders but she shrugged me off.

"I'm not a child."

"I'm not saying…"

She jumped up and pushed past me.

"Where are you going?" I asked, following along.

"Out."

"Out where?"

"Anywhere away from you!"

And she was gone.

It was pointless following her. It would just have made her more anxious, more irrational. Every time she heard news from Bosnia she would go off into a dizzy spin. I tried to keep her away from the television, away from the papers. But talk of the war was all around, and it was an impossible task.

Everything was on the move. Warships and cargo vessels were arriving off the port of Split. The warring factions were negotiating some kind of a peace deal in the USA. The Americans were planning to bridge the Sava River in Croatia's northeast. There was much talk of NATO marching into Bosnia-Herzegovina to impose order. It seemed like the bombing campaign had been successful. Perhaps they should have launched it two years before.

Isabella returned late in the evening. She looked tired and drawn, but at least she had calmed down.

"I'm sorry," she said.

We hugged and I knew things would probably be fine for a few days.

"Can't we get you to see a doctor?" I asked.

"You know I don't want that."

"Why not? You're clearly not well."

"I know."

She sat on our small settee. She looked so tiny and so frail, but also very beautiful. She drew a shawl around her shoulders, and I busied myself making her a meal that I knew she'd hardly touch.

"You look cold," I said.

"It is cold out there. Winter is really arriving."

"I wonder if they get snow down here on the coast?"

"They already have snow in the mountains," she said.

"So let's stay on the coast."

"We can't stay here forever."

I brought her through a bowl of linguine with garlic and shrimp that I'd heated through. "I'll get some wine," I said.

"That would be nice." She picked half-heartedly at the pasta.

"It's a rosé," I said. "A good one."

She drank a large measure, and nodded. "It is a good one." I poured her some more.

"When do you think we should leave?" I asked.

"In the New Year. Sooner or later the authorities will discover we're no longer in the Army. Then we'll be classified as illegal immigrants."

"We'll go back to England. More wine?"

"Yes. More wine. And yes, back to England I suppose."

"You don't sound convinced."

"The pasta is nice," she said.

I drank more wine and finished my share of the food. Isabella had barely eaten any of hers.

"Aren't you hungry, darling?" I asked.

"I could eat a horse."

"We don't have a horse," I said. I poured some more wine.

She laughed. "Then I shall eat pasta and shrimp."

But she barely finished half the bowl.

"Do we have another bottle?" she asked, presently.

"Of course."

I placed the bowls and the cutlery in the sink and left them unwashed for the morning, then pulled the cork on another bottle of rosé. We sat together on the settee and she leaned against me. The warm glow of alcohol worked its way into our blood.

"Do you think we should have children?" she asked.

"Lots of them," I said.

"Boys or girls?"

"Two of each, at least."

"Which first?"

"A boy first, then a girl. Then two more girls, and another boy."

"I thought you said two of each?"

"I changed my mind," I said. "And anyway, we were careless. The second boy arrived as a surprise."

"We planned the others?"

"It's good to have a plan."

I poured the last of the wine, and we sat together in silence for a while.

"Do you know," she said, "that we have drunk a whole bottle of wine each?"

"I do know. That's rather wonderful, isn't it?"

She snuggled against me and drained her glass. "It is rather wonderful," she said. Then she slept.

After a while I let her down gently onto the settee and covered her with the shawl and a blanket. Then I curled up on the sheepskin rug a little too drunk to care about the cold.

A bowl shattered against the kitchen wall; then another, followed by the cutlery and the cooking pot, and an empty wine bottle.

"Why didn't you wash up?" she screamed. "Why all this fucking mess?"

"Bella, don't…"

"You can't tell me what to do! Always telling me what to do!"

Her eyes were wild and staring and she had a kitchen knife in her hand. I backed away, my heart racing, my head pounding from too much wine and not enough sleep.

"Put the knife down. Please, put the knife down…"

She advanced a couple of steps, then looked down at the knife. She drew the blade deliberately across her forearm, slicing the skin. Not deep, but deep enough to part the flesh, draw blood, expose the fatty tissue below.

"Bella!" I lunged forward, but she'd dropped the blade to the floor. I grabbed her arm, applied pressure on the wound, staunched the bleeding. "Why the hell did you do that?"

But her eyes were uncomprehending, as shocked as mine. She was shaking her head, trying to say something, but the words wouldn't come. I kicked the knife away into the corner of the room and sat her on the floor, keeping her injured arm raised. I grabbed a kitchen towel and wrapped it around the wound, maintaining the pressure.

It wasn't a deep wound, not a serious wound. But this was the blood of the woman I loved, every drop of it precious, the spreading scarlet stain on the towel and the dark red droplets on the floor shocking beyond belief.

The doctor in the local health clinic was quick and efficient. The wound didn't need stitching, and within twenty minutes of arrival Isabella had been cleaned and bandaged. The doctor prescribed some tranquilisers, and after listening carefully to my story suggested that Bella should be seen by a psychiatrist because she had the symptoms of severe post-traumatic stress. But I had to tell him that she wouldn't agree to this, so he told me I should learn about this condition because left untreated it could well prove to be catastrophic for her.

I took Isabella back to our apartment and put her to bed. After several attempts I managed to connect with the Observers' staff sergeant in Split. I explained what had been happening and he agreed at once to see what he could do. I met him that evening in the reception area of our apartment building. He was carrying a couple of pamphlets and a small book.

"How is she?" he asked.

"Sleeping. They gave her some pills."

"Poor woman." He seemed genuinely concerned. The relief at having someone willing to show support must have showed in my face. "You look exhausted," he said.

"It's been tough," I said. "She's so up and down. She was great last night, but then this happens. These episodes seem to be happening more and more frequently."

"It won't stop," he said. "At least, not for a good while. She's seen a lot. So have you, as I understand things."

"Nothing like what she's seen."

"Talking together about what the pair of you have experienced might help some," he said. "But as for the rest of it, she really needs professional counselling."

"I know she does. Strange thing is, I think she knows it too. But she simply refuses to see anyone."

"Read through these. They might help."

"Thanks for bringing them here," I said.

"Least I could do. We could get her some support through the Army system, you know."

We shook hands.

"I'll let you know if she changes her mind," I said.

"You know where we are. But we won't be here forever. Things are changing up-country."

"For the better, I hope?"

He laughed. "We'll see."

Then he was gone.

I read through the pamphlets and then the book, which was a short treatise on Post Traumatic Stress Disorder published by the British Army's Command Psychology, whatever that might have been. I realised that Isabella and I did need to talk.

I bided my time and awaited the next outburst. It didn't take long. She had been hanging around the apartment all day, picking at the adhesive tape that held the bandage to her arm, smoking cigarettes and staring out from the terrace. It was as if she was awaiting the opportunity to pick a fight, anticipating a catalyst to confrontation.

I wasn't even aware of what triggered her tantrum, but when she kicked off with a screaming fit I grabbed her wrists and pulled her into the living room, forcing her to sit on the settee. She seemed so shocked at my response that her anger dissipated in a moment. She stared at me with big wide eyes. Her mouth hung open and her shoulders slumped in an attitude of total contrition.

"Why are you shouting at me?" I asked.

She mouthed a response, but no words came.

"Where do you go to when you're staring into the distance?" I continued. "Are you back in the war? Back there in Bosnia?"

"Not just Bosnia…" Her voice was small and choked. "I… so many…" And then her eyes were welling with tears and they flowed down her cheeks, so I released my grip and she buried her head in her hands.

"Where then, Bella?" I said. "If not just Bosnia, where else?"

"Here too. It's not just Bosnia. This shit has been going on all over the place…"

"Here, in Trogir?" I asked.

"Not in Trogir, but in Croatia. Before the war in Bosnia."

"You were here?"

She nodded. "Investigating war crimes."

"You saw some of those things?"

"No, I interviewed people. The families. The survivors. The mothers…" Then she was crying again, and I didn't want to push her too hard.

"We saw what the Serbs were doing in Sarajevo," I said. "It was a horror story."

"Serbs were victims too." She shot me an angry look. "Nobody has a monopoly of evil in this place."

"That's not the way the press is portraying it."

"The press is one-sided."

"So you're saying…"

"I'm not saying anything. I don't want to talk about it."

She went to stand up, but I stopped her.

"We need to talk about this, Bella. You're unwell. You should be talking with a psychiatrist about this. You cut yourself, for God's sake!"

"I didn't do that for God's sake."

"You know what I mean."

"Can I smoke?"

"If you must."

She lit-up with shaking hands, but at least her tears had stopped.

"I did see a few things during my first deployment," she said. "And the second time I was sent here too."

"So you've done three tours of duty in the Balkans?"

"Yes. Sarajevo was the third."

I was astonished. She must have done more time out here than any other member of the United Nations.

"Why on earth did you keep coming back, Bella? If you knew it to be such a screwed-up place?"

"Oh, you know. Duty, orders, excitement. It's like a drug I suppose." She drew deeply on her cigarette. "When you're there it's horrible beyond belief. But when you're away you sort of miss it. It draws you back. It drew me back. I never thought I'd come back."

She was calm now, so I pressed on.

"Why do you lose your temper so easily?" I asked.

"I don't know."

"Is it because you suddenly find yourself back there? Seeing those things? Interviewing those victims?"

"Could be."

"Then can't we find a way of avoiding those thoughts? Some kind of coping mechanism?"

"You sound like a shrink," she said.

"I hope so."

"A coping mechanism sounds like a cliché."

"It's something I read."

"Then stop reading."

"We need to talk."

"We are talking."

"We need to talk more."

"You're talking nonsense," she said.

I stood up, and for a moment was tempted to crack yet another bottle of wine. But the answer didn't lay in a bottle of wine. The answer lay in having Bella face her fears and then finding a way of negotiating herself around them; a way of distancing memory, of coping with emotion.

"What were you doing in Sarajevo when you visited the dark side?" I asked.

"You mean the Serb side?"

"Of course."

"Those are my people. It doesn't have to be called the dark side."

"Your people?"

"I'm a Serb, remember?"

"You're English," I said. "You were born in England."

"I have Serb blood in my veins."

"You have English blood in your veins."

"Not according to those idiots who called me a traitor."

"So what were you doing on the dark side, with your English blood and your Serb ethnicity?"

Then she was up and striding to and fro across the apartment, angry but trying to contain herself; anxious yet trying to hold it down.

"I won't tell you what I was doing there," she exclaimed. "It's between me and Her Majesty's Government. Exclusively."

"So you were spying?"

"I was not."

"Then you were liaising?"

"Sort of."

"Setting up deals?" I asked.

"None of your business."

"It is my business, Bella. It's my business because I love you."

That pulled her up short. She stopped her striding and stared at me for a moment.

"Yes. You do, don't you?"

I tried my little-boy-lost smile, and for a fleeting moment she responded. But then she was striding backwards and forwards again with a freshly lit cigarette between her fingers.

"I hated those people," she said. "They're evil. All of them."

"Who are?"

"Can you imagine talking to those people and sharing food with them and drinking *Slivovica* with them, and toasting the *Republika* with them and listening to their talk about the destruction of towns and cities and the deportation of hundreds of thousands of people… can you imagine having to pretend that they're not really monsters but politically legitimate and militarily responsible? That they're rational, decent human beings who can be negotiated with and influenced by fairness and rational debate?"

"Who are *they*?" I hardly needed to press the point, but I wanted to hear her say it.

"Karadzic and Mladic, and all the other creeps we were talking with over there."

"We?"

"OK, that's enough. I've said enough. I was a part of it, a small part of it, that's all you need to know."

She parked her backside on the edge of the settee, and I knew from the look on her face she'd go no further down that path.

"What about your first tour of duty over here then, your time in Croatia?" I asked. "You said you saw some horrible things."

"You need to listen more carefully," she said sharply. "I didn't *see* things; I *heard* about things."

"From victims, yes?"

"Sometimes."

"Victims of war crimes?"

"All war is a crime. You said that yourself, remember?"

"I was innocent back then."

"Weren't we all, in the beginning?"

"Tell me about those people," I said.

"I don't want to."

"Why don't you want to?"

"Because."

"Because what?"

She jumped up and headed for the door. I tried to block her way, but she bunched up, pushed past. I grabbed our coats and followed-on, taking the stairs three at a time to catch up. She was out on the street, striding away, angry but not running, almost as if she was trying to get away but didn't really want to get away.

"Tell me," I said again.

But her head was down and her lips were thin and set, so I put her coat around her shoulders and trotted along beside her. She walked blindly from street to street through the town, then across the old bridge to the mainland side as the wind played around us. I held my tongue, waiting for her to talk.

"The Croats were the worst," she said eventually, and her voice was almost a hiss, barely loud enough to hear. "They could charm you and joke with you, and convince you that you were their best friend, that everything was going to work out fine. And when they began to kill you, you would wonder how it could be that such a nice man could be doing such a thing, that surely this was all some kind of a mistake."

"That's what the survivors told you?"

"Or the relatives of victims."

"But how could they know?" I asked.

"Because they were there. They saw. The Croats *wanted* them to see."

"Wanted them to see their loved ones being killed?"

"Yes."

She was walking slower now, shivering. She let me hold her arm, and leaned into me as if for support.

"Can't you find a way of putting this down, Bella? It's not your burden. You don't need to carry it."

"I do wish... but I can't... it's just so difficult. All it takes is a sound, a word, a smell. And there I am, right back in the heart of it. Or with some mother telling me that she saw her child set on fire, or her husband shot in the head. It's like a video tape that plays and plays, over and over again."

"They should never have sent you back here."

"They didn't send me. I volunteered." She shuddered, and I knew she was crying again.

"There is something else, isn't there?" I asked.

She nodded.

"Something that makes you feel you're somehow personally responsible for these things? Was it the things you saw at Ahmici?"

She stiffened. Stopped walking. Looked at me.

"There was a young Muslim girl," she said, hesitantly, quietly. "Just a teenager. She'd slipped into the woods before the Croats arrived. We found her hiding under a pile of logs. Took care of her, got her out of there. I became her best friend, kind of a big sister and surrogate mother rolled into one. We hid her until we figured a way to get her through Croat held territory and into Sarajevo."

"A Schindler's operation?"

"We hadn't really started all that back then. But yes, I suppose it was a forerunner. The mistake we made was trusting other people to get her through."

"What happened?"

She was silent for a moment.

"The girl was passed from one location to another. The idea was to get her onto an aid convoy and into the city where she'd be safer. But something went wrong, and she ended up being stuck for a couple of days in a farmhouse near Kiseljak. We couldn't stay with her. And then they found her."

"The Croats?"

"Yes."

"What happened to her?" I hardly needed to ask the question.

"She was gang-raped. Just like those poor people coming out of Srebrenica were raped. They didn't kill her though. We found her the next day, but she was in a terrible state. We got her into a safe house then headed to Kiseljak to fetch a doctor."

She was clinging to me now, crying bitterly. I hugged her, knowing she had to finish the story. She took a deep breath, took control.

"When we got back, she was dead," she said, matter-of-factly. "She'd hung herself with her own headscarf. I guess the shame was too much for her to bear. By then she must have realised that the rest of her family had been killed, though we never told her."

"You saw her body?" I asked.

Bella looked at me with wide, sad eyes. "I found her," she said. "Her face was purple, her tongue was swollen and covered with flies. But it was the smell. I can't forget the smell…"

I held her tight. There was nothing else I could do.

"You believed it was your fault?"

She sobbed, a shuddering, wretched release of emotion. "I should never have left her."

We stood together in silence until her tears were spent.

"Shall we go home?" I asked, presently.

"Yes. Please."

So we walked slowly back to the apartment and I lay with her in bed as she fell into a fitful sleep. The early winter wind played around the terrace and the sea lapped against the harbour wall, and I wondered how we could build on this small beginning.

CHAPTER 30

I was surprised at how cool the weather was getting here on the Adriatic coast. I had always imagined it to be much warmer down by the sea. But I supposed that at least it was warmer than spending winter in Sarajevo. We didn't see any frost, but the temperature at night couldn't have been much above freezing. When the wind blew, it was uncomfortably cold.

I often saw the fisherman, sat on the harbour wall mending his nets or preparing his lines. He would be wearing the same thin jacket that he was using when I first met him, and his gnarled hands seemed impervious to the cold.

"You should move your boat back to Korcula," he said one day. "That little mooring might not hold in a storm."

I mentioned this to Isabella and she brightened up immediately. "We could sail her there," she said. "One last voyage before winter."

So I made plans for us to sail the yacht to Korcula, which was less than a hundred miles away. It would be good to have a break from our tiny apartment, and I knew that the fisherman's brother would help us haul the boat out of the water and secure her safely onshore for the winter.

It took me a week to prepare the boat. Each time I left the apartment I felt a little anxious because Isabella was still up and down, though she was mostly up. But I couldn't be by her side for every moment of every day.

I worked quickly on the yacht; storing her for up to a week even though we could probably make the distance in little more than a single day if we felt the need for speed. I checked her sails, filled her water tank, topped-off her fuel and made sure that her safety equipment was serviceable. Next season we would carry a liferaft and maybe invest in a VHF radio. But she was a fine yacht, strong and seaworthy. We'd pick a hole in the weather, plan our trip with safety in mind. Everything would be fine.

The day before we were due to leave, Isabella went missing. I searched the usual places. Down by the fish harbour, along the out-of-season picturesque waterfront, up by the cathedral where she'd taken to hanging around late in the evenings. But I couldn't find her.

I managed to get a call through to the staff sergeant, but the Observers were far too busy to be of any use. NATO was planning to deploy with force into Bosnia-Herzegovina, he said. Everything else was a sideshow, this was a massive movement of logistics and his hands were full. So I asked the fisherman to help me search the streets and we ranged around through the night, but Isabella Harris was nowhere to be found.

"Maybe she just needs some time alone," said the old man. "Perhaps you should just wait in your house. I'm sure she will come home."

So I waited, and found myself smoking some of her cigarettes and burying my face into her pillow to smell her fragrance. I fell asleep and fell through a dream into a nightmare, a nightmare where the streets were running with blood and a body was twitching in the gutter and a woman was scrubbing at the ground with a coarse-haired brush and Bella was curled up against a wall screaming and crying.

Then I awoke and she was there, and she looked like death and was indeed screaming at me. I rolled from the bed and wondered if I was still in the nightmare, But no, this was real, and there was hate in her eyes and froth on her lips, and her lips were blue with the cold and she had that goddam kitchen knife in her hand.

"Why?" she screamed. "Why did you make me go there?"

"Go where?"

"You know where! To the market, why did you make me go to the market?"

"I didn't make you…"

"The fuck you didn't make me! You made me go there, you made me go there and I didn't want to go there, and you made me go, and everything was fucked up and it was because of you…"

"Bella, you're not making any sense… put the knife down…"

She was walking around the room with the knife in her hand. I had to get the knife. I knew what she did with the knife.

"Come on darling, calm down," I said.

"You made me go, you made me… you *knew* I didn't want to go…"

"I didn't know, I swear…"

I had to get the knife.

She circled the room, eyeing me sideways, pointing the knife towards me. Her eyes were dark-rimmed and her hair was matted and wet. I could see that she was shivering and that her clothes were soaked through and that she must have been in the sea. My mind was whirling and I had to get the knife, I knew what she did with the knife, she had to be saved from the knife…

"I wanted to go away," she continued. "But you wanted to go to the market. I *knew* what would happen, but you had to go to the market. And everything went wrong, just like before, exactly like before, and you *ran* towards the market and I ran after you, I tried to stop you, I didn't want you to see, but you *saw*, and I saw, and it was just like before and there were dead people… those poor, poor people…"

She was biting on her knuckles. I could see blood. Her eyes were crazed and I moved closer to her and she waved the knife towards my face so I kept my hands open and my arms wide but she continued to circle and I matched her step by step; and now it seemed like a ballet or a bullfight, a macabre dance of death.

"Give me the knife," I said, gently.

She sucked on her knuckles and looked at the knife and looked at her arm and looked at the knife again, and then stared me straight in the eye.

"You *made* me do it," she declared, defiantly. She stopped circling. Stood still. Held the blade against her wrist.

But I was close enough to strike, twist her arm away. She went down and I had the knife. I threw the knife and she was undamaged, and the knife was on the floor and it span into the far corner of the room.

We lay there for several minutes, panting. I did not let go of her arms. I pinned her with my bodyweight. Then all her strength was gone and we held each other and we cried with each other, until daylight brought a little warmth to the apartment and I was quite sure that the crisis had passed.

CHAPTER 31

The morning rain was sheeting across the water and the light in our bedroom was pale and pleasant. Our thin blanket covered us and wrapped us and the pillows were soft under our heads as we breathed the salt-laden air and climbed slowly from the depths of our sleep.

Isabella was still in my arms. She was calm and soft and her breathing was regular. There was no reason to think that anything might be wrong in her world or wayward in her mind. But she was fractured and lost, traumatised beyond pain.

We had to find a way of coping with all of this. I had to persuade her to seek help, embrace professional advice. I knew now that there was only so much I could do. I believed she loved me, but love might not be enough. Sooner or later she would fall and there would be nothing I could do to prevent it happening.

She stirred and turned towards me. Her eyes opened and there was warmth and love. I kissed her cheek and she purred like a kitten.

"You look tired," she said, and it was strange to me that she never seemed to have morning breath.

"I am tired."

"You need a shave."

"Yes, I do."

She stretched her slender legs, and seemed surprised that she was still fully clothed.

"Was I a little crazy last night?" she asked.

"You were a little crazy. I had to be firm with you."

"I like it when you are firm."

"We have to get you help, Bella. When you are crazy, it can be dangerous. You try to hurt yourself."

"I don't want any help. You can help. You always help." She pouted like a little child, then smiled broadly and rolled out of bed. "I'll make breakfast," she said.

I wasn't concerned, because I had thrown all our knives from the terrace into the sea.

We took a long walk through the rain later in the day, and the raindrops bounced from the cobbles and splashed in the puddles all along the deserted streets and across the lonely quay.

Isabella told me that she was feeling fine, that I needn't worry because it was all out of her system now. She said that she was sorry and that she'd gone for a swim in the sea last night and it had made her realise that the answer to all of this was to put all her bad thoughts in one compartment of her mind and lock the door and throw away the key.

So I told her if ever any of those troubles managed to break free then she must come and tell me straight away so we could grab them and catch them and lock them up again before they could do any mischief; and I wondered if her talk of control and compartments and keys was just some kind of a smokescreen intended to calm me down and divert my attention from watching over her.

So I took special care to watch over her with more diligence that ever before. I looked carefully for signs of anxiety or anger or pain, but she did seem to steadily improve. Perhaps her latest outburst had provided some relief, allowed some of the poison to escape. As the days passed by she certainly seemed to be in a lighter frame of mind. She began to eat well, and I could see a strength and vitality returning to her that had been absent for so long.

Occasionally she did go missing, but invariably I found her sat on the cathedral steps smoking a cigarette, deep in thought. I once asked if she'd found God, but she just laughed and told me that she found it peaceful in this place and that she was certainly not a Catholic.

"When will we take the boat to Korcula?" she asked one particularly stormy morning as heavy rain hammered on the terrace and thick clouds rolled across the sky.

"You still want to do that?"

"Of course."

"Not while the weather is so bad," I said. "But everything is ready. All we need is a few fine days."

"Let's do it as soon as the weather breaks," she said.

"OK."

"I'm sorry for all the trouble I give you."

"You don't need to be sorry, Bella."

"You're a wonderful person, darling. You take such good care of me."

"I'd be lost without you."

She hugged me.

"We have had some adventures together, haven't we?" she asked.

"Yes. We have. And we'll have many more in the future. And we shall have five babies."

"Not just yet, darling. We're too young for children."

"I feel like I'm fifty."

"You poor sweetheart." She kissed me on the cheek. "Do I have that effect on you?"

"It's not just you. We had a rough time in Bosnia."

"Not as rough as all those poor people."

"That's true."

"I do want to go sailing. We will go, won't we?" There was a keen urgency in her voice.

"Yes, of course we will. As soon as the weather is right."

"It will be soon. I know it will. And we'll have a lovely time."

"I hope so."

"I know we will."

The weather improved, and a few days later shortly after first light the fisherman took us out to the *Balkan Princess* with our little inflatable dinghy in tow. "Remember that the weather can turn bad very quickly," he said as we clambered onboard the yacht.

"We'll be careful," I said. "We'll have your brother get in touch when we've safely arrived."

"Have fun!" He threw a small bag into the cockpit. "Some fish for dinner!"

We thanked him and waved as he powered the outboard and steered back towards the harbour. I realised in that moment that he was the only real friend we'd had in this place, apart from the staff sergeant, maybe.

It didn't take long to pull the dinghy onto the foredeck, lash her down and stow the last of our things below. The fish was packed in ice so I placed it in a bucket, and tied-off the bucket in the cockpit so the fish didn't stink out the cabin. Then we hoisted the mainsail, slipped our mooring and bore away with the wind until we were clear of the harbour. Then I rolled out the genoa as our little ship settled onto a comfortable broad reach.

It would only take a couple of hours to clear the island on our starboard side. Then we could shape a course south towards the narrow shipping lane between the islands of Solta and Brac, and from there we'd have a few hours of exposed offshore sailing to the ancient port of Hvar. I was hopeful we'd be there before last light.

"This is wonderful," exclaimed Isabella, tugging gently on the tiller every time the yacht tried to round-up.

"Yes, it is," I said.

It was wonderful. Wonderful to see Bella with a smile on her face and a red flush on her cheeks; wonderful to see the sunlit hills of the coast slip by; wonderful to feel the fresh wind in our faces, and to smell the sea and listen to the sails straining on their sheets.

I busied myself around the yacht, securing everything that was still rolling around and generally snugging her down for the offshore passage. Everything would become more dynamic when we cleared the lee of the island. Then we'd have to watch out for ships plying to and from the commercial port in Split. We had a small radar reflector positioned high on our mast, so hopefully we'd be clearly visible to passing vessels. But the *Balkan Princess* was a tiny target to spot from the bridge of a large ship even though she had a bright yellow hull, and we'd need to remain alert.

I poured two mugs of hot coffee from a flask and joined Isabella on the helm. The sails were nicely set and didn't need much trimming. My hands were cold and hers were pure white, but the coffee warmed us both. I took over the helm and she snuggled in behind me to get some shelter from the wind.

I thought that we must get hold of some proper oilskins, and then remembered that we should be using safety harnesses and lifejackets. So I went below and dug them out, and we struggled to fit them. But then it was done and we were safely clipped-on to the yacht, and the end of the island was approaching fast.

We rounded the point and hardened-up onto a beat. The wind was in the southwest and a little stronger now that we were clear of the land, but in any case hardening into the wind increased its apparent speed across the deck and the wind chill kicked-in with a vengeance.

We pulled on gloves and zipped our waterproof jackets as high as they'd go. The boat heeled sharply on her new heading and spray chipped over her windward bow, soaking us and freezing us and blinding us. Isabella shrieked with delight and I grimaced in discomfort, but our little boat shaped a true course for the gap between the islands ahead and I knew that once we were through, the seas would be bigger and we'd have to harden up even more to safely clear the western tip of Hvar Island.

Our little boat ploughed on gamely, taking each wave in her stride, soaking us time and again with freezing cold spray. An outbound ship passed close down our port side like a huge apartment block. Two more, inbound, passed us further off, one of them a warship of some description but bearing no ensign. We saw nobody on the bridge-wings, and could only wonder if we'd been spotted on radar. But they were a safe distance off.

By the time we reached the gap between the islands my back was sore and my hands were numb, and in truth I did feel a little queasy. But Isabella seemed to be having a great time. I could barely see her eyes, but she hugged me hard every time a larger wave hit the bow, and she would duck down behind me to spare herself from the worst of the spray. I squeezed her leg and she pinched my waist.

It was fine to be so alive, and so cold.

We took a reef in the main and furled the genoa accordingly a mile or so before reaching the gap. The gap itself wasn't anything like as narrow as it had seemed on the chart. In reality it was about a half-mile wide, but there was still a funnelling of wind and we encountered a few breaking seas that slammed into the yacht as solid walls of water, heeling her over to an impossible angle and twisting her around on her side. But each time she recovered gamely and we pulled on the tiller to bring her bow back up and fill the sails.

Then we were through, and at once could feel a longer, almost oceanic swell under the keel. The sea was a deeper blue here, and the breeze wasn't as strong as I'd feared. The yacht settled into a steady rhythm, harder on the wind for sure, but somehow sweeter. She was no longer throwing spray across her decks.

The island of Hvar was fine on our port bow, and even from this distance I could see waves breaking in spectacular fashion at the foot of its westernmost point.

"Do you think we'll make it?" asked Isabella, pulling down her hood.

"If we don't, we'll have to tack off to the northwest for a couple of miles, then tack back again. Which means we'd arrive in the dark."

"That doesn't sound good."

"It will be OK. But I'd rather arrive in daylight. We'll see."

"Do you want something to eat?" she asked.

"There are some sandwiches down below."

"You don't want fish?"

"I do not want fish, thank you." I'd been very conscious of the smell these past few hours.

"I'll get the sandwiches."

So we ate sandwiches and drank cold water from plastic bottles, and the island ahead drew closer. But all the time the wind forced us nearer to that maelstrom of breaking waves at the foot of the cliff.

Just when I was about to tack the yacht away to the northwest, the wind freed a little and I knew we were going to make it around the point. We weathered the western tip of the island with several hundred yards to spare, watching the splendid power of the sea breaking with explosive force against the cliffs, glad not to be facing a harbour approach in the dark, keen to see this passage over and done.

We reached along the coast and in the fading light of late afternoon handed the mainsail and furled away the genoa to approach the port of Hvar under engine power. We motored slowly into the bay and dropped anchor a few hundred yards off the town quay. The place struck me as looking very similar to Trogir. We were the only sailing yacht in the harbour.

CHAPTER 32

"What are you doing here?"

The policeman had that look of a man who, knowing he bears authority, requires the tremulous, undivided attention of anyone he questions. He stood with a hand on his gun and the thumb of his other hand hooked over his belt. His chin had a few days' growth, his stomach had seen a few too many beers, and his eyes were narrow with suspicion.

"We are taking our boat to Korcula," I said.

"Korcula?"

"Yes, it's the island over there." I pointed towards the east. I didn't mean it to sound sarcastic, but I suppose my response could have been interpreted that way.

The policeman's grip on his gun seemed to tighten. "How many of you are there?"

"There are two of us."

"Where is this other person?"

"She's on the yacht."

"She? You are married?"

"No, we are friends," I said.

"Passport."

I handed him my passport.

"British?"

"That's what it says."

"What are you doing here?" he asked.

This was tedious.

"Taking our boat to Korcula…"

"Yes, you told me that. I mean, what are you doing here in Croatia?"

It did seem like a fair question.

"We're on holiday," I replied.

"Here, in Croatia?"

"Yes. It's a lovely place."

"Even with the war?"

"The war is over, isn't it? Wasn't it finished in Croatia years ago?"

"We don't see many tourists here in Hvar. Not yet. Not like before the war."

"It is a very lovely place," I said. "I'm sure things will improve."

He handed me back my passport.

"I will need to see the woman's too," he said.

"I can bring it to you."

"She will need to bring it. I will wait here."

It seemed pointless protesting. I jumped into the dinghy and untied the line. Within a few minutes I was onboard the *Balkan Princess,* and my own princess was stirring in her bunk.

"I have bread and pastries and fresh milk for breakfast," I said. "And there is a lovely little restaurant on the quay that serves grilled sardines for lunch. It has a good wine list, too."

"Lovely!" Isabella was rubbing her eyes. "What's the time?"

"Time to get up," I said. "Put on a smile. Some horrid policeman ashore wants to see your passport."

But she didn't put on a smile. She didn't seem pleased at all. She pulled on her clothes without saying a word and climbed into the dinghy with a scowl on her face. I rowed us towards the quay, and the policeman was stood there with another man in uniform, but a different uniform, and the new man had a clipboard in his hand. I tied off the dinghy and we stepped ashore. Neither of the men offered to help.

"Passport." Isabella handed hers over. The policeman looked at me. "Yours too."

He flicked through them, and then handed them to the man with the clipboard.

"Why are you here?" asked the policeman.

"I've already told you…" I began, but he interrupted.

"Not you. Her."

"We're on our boat," said Isabella. "Sailing to Korcula."

"Why are you with this man?"

"That's none of your business."

The policeman stared at her and then said something to his colleague. The other man nodded and glanced up at Isabella. She held his stare, and after a moment he looked away.

"This man is from the Immigration Department," said the policeman. "I will translate for him."

"That's fine," I said. "What does he need to know?"

They talked between themselves, and the policeman asked a series of banal questions concerning our port of departure, our current address in Trogir, how long we intended staying in Croatia and whether we had enough money to buy air tickets back to the UK. The Immigration official wrote everything on a form attached to his clipboard, then had us sign. I asked what the form was, and the policeman told me it was a landing card.

I held out my hand for the passports, but he told me they'd be kept until the Customs Department had checked the status of the yacht and that meanwhile we were not to try and leave the harbour and that we would be arrested if we did. The pair muttered between themselves and then sneered at Isabella. They left, and we returned to the yacht in silence.

Isabella Harris was fuming.

"What did they say?" I asked, lighting the gas cooker to brew up some coffee.

"You don't want to know."

"Yes I do."

"They said I'm probably your whore." She was slumped on her cabin berth. "I hate these people. They're all the same. Give them a uniform and they think they can do whatever they like."

"They're just doing their job, Bella," I said, trying to keep her anger from rising. "They may be obnoxious, but they're probably right to check us out."

"I hate them."

"I love that you hate them."

"You do?"

"I love everything about you."

"Really?"

"Yes. Really."

"Did you just put that bread in the oven?" she asked.

"I did."

"It smells heavenly."

"Can we throw away the fish?" I asked. "I can smell it from here."

"I think we should," she replied.

So we threw away the fish and poured the coffee. But I could see there was still a dark scowl on Bella's beautiful, rosy-cheeked face.

We waited three days for the return of our passports, but a delay would have been inevitable in any case. The wind picked-up through the rest of that day, and by the following morning it was howling a full gale from the north complete with flurries of snow and frost on the deck.

We rode to our tiny anchor as the *Balkan Princess* tugged on the cable like an angry terrier pulls on its leash. I knew if the wind backed or veered to the south we could be in big trouble. With wind in the north we had the lee of the land, but with it in the south we'd have been terribly exposed to waves sweeping through the harbour and crashing past us onto a leeward shore.

We huddled for warmth on the cabin sole with bunk cushions beneath and sleeping bags wrapped all around, but there was little comfort to be found. Gradually, incrementally, the weather deteriorated and we succumbed to the inevitable onset of seasickness. It was cold and miserable, tedious and awful. All the things I'd not wanted this cruise to be.

As early daylight filtered into the cabin next morning, I resolved to abandon our boat whilst we still could. So we launched the tender and I clambered onboard over the heaving, pitching rail. Bella joined me moments later, clinging onto the side of the yacht as spray soaked us through and salt water stung our eyes. We struggled to untie the line and set ourselves free, but then we were away towards the shore, our tiny floating home left in our wake and the refuge of a warm hotel ahead.

The worst of the storm blew through that afternoon. By early evening everything had calmed down and the skies were beginning to clear. I dug into our cash reserves and treated us to a fine meal in a small and intimate bistro, but Isabella was morose and uncommunicative.

We drank a little too much wine and headed back early to our hotel, a small yet comfortable establishment overlooking the harbour. We lay together and made unsatisfactory love in that awkward way you do when there are unresolved issues to be dealt with. I tried to make her talk, share her feelings, but she was sullen and withdrawn. We slept back to back, and I awoke before first light to see her once again sat on a chair, staring at the wall and smoking a cigarette.

Our passports were returned without ceremony and with no explanation for the delay. We were free to leave, so we bought a small supply of fresh vegetables and fruit from a local store and rowed the dinghy off to the *Balkan Princess*. The yacht was in a horrible state below, so we cleaned ship and stowed things away ready for our passage to Korcula. The distance was only about forty miles, and with the wind now in the west I was hopeful we'd make it before last light. The seas had eased considerably.

We departed Hvar on a broad reach with a single reef in the main and all sheets eased, angling towards the island of Scedro about fifteen miles to our east. The crests of breaking waves appeared dazzlingly white against the deep blue of the Adriatic, and as our little boat raised her bow to the sea, Isabella's mood seemed to lift.

"This is lovely," she declared. Her hair was billowing in the breeze and her legs were braced against the rolling of the yacht.

"It is, isn't it?" I replied, and couldn't help grinning at her change of attitude. "Are you glad we decided to do this?"

"Of course I am, Captain."

So I went below and prepared a solid lunch for us to enjoy over the top of the day, smiling to myself that it appeared I had at last become an officer, and a Captain at that.

CHAPTER 33

The Rigid Inflatable must have been lurking in the lee of Scedro. We didn't see it coming. The men onboard must have watched us bowl past, then powered offshore to come upon us directly from astern.

The first I knew of its presence was hearing *Oh my God!* from Isabella, and then the roar of powerful engines and the shouting of angry men. I scrambled towards the cockpit but they were already onboard, roughly shoving Bella from the helm then pushing violently past me to check out the cabin, all machine guns and wetsuits and radios and energy. There was no time to evade, no sense in resisting. These men were on a mission.

The inflatable dropped astern, crushing our guardwires and tearing away the navigation light mounted on our stern. Four men had boarded us, four men with no discernible badges of rank or other means of identification, four men with guns and bullets and knives and attitude. I tried to ask who they were and what they wanted, but one of them thumped me hard in the chest with the butt of his MP5 and I collapsed into the cockpit well.

Then Isabella Harris was up and at them, clawing at the men's eyes, screaming in Serbo-Croat, pushing aside their guns and taking them on. I tried to stop her but was hit again, and then they had her pinned to the deck as the yacht rounded-up and the sails collapsed and we were wallowing with everything taken aback by the wind.

I shouted, "Bella, don't..."

But she was screaming at them and they were screaming at her. She bit one of them on the hand and he yelled in pain then punched her in the face; so I shook off the shock and leaped on him in turn, and there was a fury of energy and fists and steel and cold, solid seawater washing into the cockpit as the boat rolled and yawed like a stricken beast.

Then everything was under control and the pair of us were plasticuffed, hog-tied and pinned to the deck as the men in black rifled through the cabin and pointed their guns at us and threw our belongings over the side into the turbulent sea as their Rigid Inflatable circled like a menacing predator shark.

"Where are you going?" asked one of the men whom I took to be the leader, because he spoke English and was asking the question.

"Korcula."

"Why?"

"To leave our yacht there for the winter."

Isabella said something in Serbo-Croat, but he pushed her with his boot. "Shut up, bitch!"

"Leave her alone..."

"You want I should have my men fuck her?"

"I'll kill you..."

He laughed. "How is that?" He said something to his men, and they laughed too. "You are British?" He had our passports.

"You can see we are."

"You should not be here."

"We're just delivering our yacht…"

"You should not be here with your yacht. It is not allowed."

"Should not be where?"

"Here, anywhere. There is a war."

"The war is over."

"It will never be over."

Isabella was struggling to hold herself in. I could see it in her eyes and in the downturn of her tightly drawn mouth. I could see blood in her mouth. I had to stop her from speaking.

"This is ridiculous," I said. "We're just sailing our yacht to Korcula."

"Where did you come from? We know you've been to Hvar."

"Trogir. We sailed from Trogir."

"Then you must go back there."

"Why?"

He grabbed me by the chest and pulled me close. "Because I am telling you to go back there."

"But…"

"Or we can cut your woman up, shoot you both in the head, and then sink your boat. Your choice, my friend." His voice was no more than a hiss, and his eyes had that dead look of a man totally certain of his ability to do exactly what he says he will do. He pushed me back to the deck. "Your woman. Why does she speak Serbo-Croat?"

"She was an interpreter with the United Nations."

"A spy?"

"An interpreter."

"Maybe we should shoot her anyway."

The Rigid Inflatable pulled alongside. He motioned to his men and they climbed onboard. He pulled a knife and freed my wrists. Fixed my eyes with that sightless stare. Reached down, pulled Bella's head back and held his knife to her throat.

"Take your woman and go back to Trogir," he said. "If we see you again we won't be so forgiving."

"I'll do that." My eyes were brimming with tears.

He let go of Isabella's hair, climbed over the rail and then they were gone.

I freed Bella's wrists, hugged her for ten long minutes, then shortened sail and headed our little yacht into wind to begin the long beat home.

CHAPTER 34

The slog to windward would take us deep into the night and I could see no prospect of raising Trogir until the following afternoon. I secured everything as best I could and Isabella helped a little, but I could see that she'd become bitterly morose and I feared for her frame of mind. Nothing I could say or do raised a smile, and she responded lethargically or not at all to questions and instructions.

Late in the afternoon she threw a complete anger fit, screaming at me and crying and cursing the officials in Hvar and the men from the Rigid Inflatable. Then she threw herself onto the leeward bunk down below and seemed to descend into a near-coma.

I tried rousing her with coffee and even pinched her to solicit a reaction, but she remained inert and unresponsive. There was dried blood on her cheek. I checked several times to make sure she was still breathing, but couldn't leave the cockpit for long because the yacht was struggling to windward and every time I left the helm we lost precious ground towards our destination.

Around midnight, with the seas easing a little and our tiny navigation lights illuminating each incoming wave green to starboard and red to port, Bella suddenly appeared in the companionway with a sandwich in her hand and a smile on her tired face that I could faintly see in the pale moonlight. She had washed the blood away, though her lips were swollen and bruised.

"This is for you, darling," she said.

"Are you OK?"

"Yes, just tired. But you must be exhausted." She climbed into the cockpit and settled in front of me. "Cuddle me for a while. Then you must go and get some sleep."

"Are you sure?"

"Yes, I'll be fine. I'm better now."

"Those men are bastards."

"Yes, they are." She reached up and stroked my face. "A lot of men are bastards, darling. But not you. You're sweet."

I bent forward and kissed her damaged lips. "So are you, Bella."

"I am, aren't I?"

"Yes, you are."

"I do love you."

"I know. You told me before."

"I'll always love you."

We sat for a while and I ate the sandwich. The wind eased and the helm became easier to handle. I shook out a reef and unfurled a little more of the genoa.

"I'll take an hour," I said. "Make sure you wake me."

"Just an hour?"

"That's all I need."

"I'll wake you," she said. "I promise."

She took over the helm, then hugged me hard.

"One hour," I said.

"Goodnight, sweetheart."

I could have sworn there was a tear in her eye.

The earliest light of day was cracking the eastern horizon when Isabella woke me. I glanced at my watch. "You let me sleep this long?"

"I wanted to make sure you had a good rest," she said.

"We may have beat a little too far west."

"It doesn't matter."

"It doesn't?"

"I wish we could stay out here forever," she said.

"Wrong time of year for a long offshore passage. In the spring, maybe?"

"Maybe." She was back on the helm. "Could you make me a hot drink?"

"Sure."

I filled the kettle and lit the gas. Put the kettle on the stove. Rinsed a couple of mugs in the sink. Poked my head out of the companionway to ask Bella if she'd like something to eat.

She was gone.

I knew in an instant what she had done.

I threw myself onto the tiller and pushed the helm hard down. The yacht tacked sharply through the eye of the wind and her headsail backed. I brought the tiller hard up and lashed it to the rail. The little ship stalled, perfectly hove-to, fore-reaching gently across the oncoming waves.

She had to be close, she couldn't be far; less than a minute, *less than a minute...*

I stood on the cockpit seat, clinging to the backstay, peering desperately into the gloom of a sickly grey dawn. The seas were no longer tumbling and the wind was easing away. The cold cut through my clothes but I was already numb with fear.

I couldn't have lost her. *This was utterly wrong.*

A shaft of bright yellow sunlight cracked the horizon. Something glinted in the water, a hundred yards or so off the port quarter. I screwed my eyes tight against the sun, and there it was again.

It had to be her. There was nothing else out there.

No time to think. No time to consider. There was nothing else to be done. I dived into the ocean and swam.

The cold took my breath away, but I powered through the waves. Already my clothes were heavy. I rose on a crest, and there it was again; something tangible and solid on the surface of the sea. I doubled my effort, teeth clenched, eyes wide open.

Closer... it was her, it *had* to be her...

And then she was gone, just a few yards away.

So close... so cruel...

I trod water and caught my breath, shivering violently. The yacht blew down towards me, rising to a wave, sunlight reflecting off her sails. I turned and turned, straining to see all around.

Please don't leave me Bella, please don't leave...

But she had gone, and in minutes the sea would claim me too and I didn't care. But I struck out for the yacht anyway, legs cramping, tears mingling with the salt of the sea to blind my eyes, heart pounding fit to burst.

This was senseless, it could not be true.

My hand reached for the boat's transom and I clung on, riding with her. I hauled myself up and could see into the cabin, feel its warmth and its comfort. Just one more effort and all would be well.

I knew I was staring at a choice between life and death.

Time slowed and my shivering stopped. The stern of my gallant little ship rose and fell to the rhythm of the sea, the sea that Bella has chosen as her place to rest, the sea that should claim me too.

There was really no choice. The story had run its course. All I had to do was slip away. The stern rose one last time and a stone-cold certainty settled upon my heart. I let go of the *Balkan Princess* and turned my face towards the deep.

And there she was, in the water alongside me. Floating, breathing, but barely alive; her eyes wide open and as grey as the sea.

EPILOGUE

A cool, early summer breeze was ruffling the lace curtains, bringing a sweet smell of English country flowers into the bedroom. I closed the window, taking care with the latch, not wanting to wake her. But she stirred anyway, so I sat on the bed and took her hand and kissed her cheek. She opened her eyes and her pupils adjusted to the light of day, momentarily confused, then relaxing but still full of sleep.

"Is it time to get up?" she asked, sleepily.

"If you want to."

"I don't think so."

"Then you can sleep some more," I said.

"I already slept some more."

"Then you can get up."

"I don't want to get up." She squeezed my hand. "Lie here with me."

I kicked off my slippers and lay beside her, still holding her hand, my early morning body cold against her warm, naked skin. She pushed her backside towards me and we cuddled like that.

My body warmed up, and her hair was in my face, tickling my nose. I squeezed her from time to time as the sun rose over the trees and the morning birds chased each other and fought with each other over the seeds and breadcrumbs that I knew her mother would already have spread on the lawn.

The first bus of the day passed along the country lane close outside our window. Soon the postman would arrive and Bella's mother would knock on our door to offer tea and toast, or porridge, or bacon and eggs; or an offer to leave us in peace if we wanted, to while away the morning alone.

The dogs would bark and the cat would sneak in through the crack of the door and jump onto our bed, purring and clawing at the blanket as if asking us to move along and leave a warm space where she could curl into a ball and luxuriate in singular repose as only a cat can do.

Isabella stirred.

I gently swept her hair over her ear and asked if she would like breakfast in bed this morning. But she said no, and didn't I remember that we'd promised her mother we would go into town with her today? So we really should get out of bed and be ready for that, because her mother had been so kind and understanding. And anyway, we had to renew the prescription at the pharmacy because the medication really did help, and didn't I know just how much she loved me?

So I told her that of course I knew just how much she loved me, after all that had happened and all that we'd been through how could she ever have doubted that I knew, even for a moment?

And she said that she was only teasing, and then she was awake and stretching and yawning and rolling back the bedclothes and showing the perfect symmetry of her body. But there was no chance of pushing the issue because her mother would be knocking on that door at any moment and the dogs would be barking and the cat would be clawing, and damn it if she didn't jump out of bed and run into the bathroom before I could grab her and hold her and hug her.

It was love that had saved Bella's life that day in the Adriatic. Tried three times she'd tried to force herself beneath the waves and breathe water into her lungs. Surfaced each time because her body had refused to obey the fractured logic of her mind.

Then she'd seen the *Balkan Princess* bearing down towards her. Had seen me on the stern. Watched me dive into the sea. Realised in that instant that love can transcend fear and overcome despair.

So she'd tried calling my name but was too weak to shout. Tried swimming towards me but had no strength. Cried bitter tears of regret as the cold numbed her mind and her life ebbed away. Then awoke in my arms under the stern of our little ship.

Now we were here, living in a haven of peace and tranquillity, deep in the English countryside. Dealing with each day as it came, repairing the pain, moving forward with our lives.

I sometimes wondered how many others had been damaged this way by war. Bosnia wasn't our war, of course, but we'd made it our war. She'd made it hers by caring about everyone, an impossible load; I'd made it mine by caring about her, and by caring about the young girl, Katarina.

I did still remember Katarina, and wondered from time to time about the fate of her family.

Later that morning we drove into town, past thatched-roof cottages and green meadows and flowering hedgerows. The farmers had been sowing the land and the roads were strewn with mud where tractors had been driving across freshly ploughed fields. The air was a haze of pollen and dust, that curious mix of country and farm and summer heat that stings the eyes and tickles the throat.

"I'm going to the chemist," said Bella. "Are you going to check the post office?"

"Yes."

"Let's meet in the cathedral shop for lunch."

"Sounds good."

I kissed her on the cheek and told her that I loved her. I always did this when we parted, even if it was just for a short moment. And she always looked at me with her lovely eyes that crinkled at the corner when she smiled, and would kiss me too.

Isabella knew nothing about the post office box. It was something I used for the delivery of mail that she didn't need to see. I checked it once a week. It was my window back into the world we'd left behind, one more way of trying to isolate her from the pain of memory and reduce her anxiety into bite-sized chunks.

The box had its usual bits and pieces. A pension statement, a circular from the Inland Revenue, a couple of junk mail catalogues. But on that day there was also a handwritten letter that I tore open and read as I walked towards the cathedral. Its words stopped me dead in the street.

It was from an old colleague, who wanted to meet.

The geese in St James' Park were hissing and squabbling over chunks of bread being thrown into the lake by an old woman and there was a distant hum of traffic headed down the Mall towards Buckingham Palace. Bright sunlight was casting dappled shadows on the ground and tourists were parading along the paths with cameras hung from their necks and guidebooks clutched in their hands. Summer was taking hold in London. Wimbledon would soon be upon us and the cricket season was in full swing.

The Observers' warrant officer had changed very little, though years had passed. This was the first time I'd seen him out of uniform. It seemed a lifetime since we'd parted at the tunnel entrance in Sarajevo. Now, without his uniform, he appeared to be smaller, less imposing. It seemed so incongruous to be walking here with this man. He belonged to a different place. A place of perennially grey skies, a place of sorrow and pain.

"So why did you want to meet?" I asked. "It's been a long time."

He looked at me as if judging my mood, perhaps unsure if whatever he had to say would be well received. I made to give him some reassurance, but he began to talk. Rapidly, as if giving orders; quiet, yet intense.

"It was a crazy time after you left Sarajevo," he said. "Even crazier than before. The Serbs just went nuts, shooting-up anything that moved. The Bosnians went onto the offensive. We still had people trying to get into the city from Srebrenica and Žepa, Goražde too. Refugees. A lot of them didn't make it. Many are still missing. We never forgot about your friends in Žepa. We hit on the Red Cross almost every day, when it was safe to head across town. Every time we went there, the lists were longer. Lists of the dead, lists of the living. But there was no word on your friends, good or bad."

"And now?"

"I'll come to that. How are you dealing with Bella?" he asked, and I had to think about this for a moment.

"It's really been a case of breaking her memories down into single events, then dealing with each event in turn."

"You get her to talk about them?"

"Yes. I walk her through the experience, and wherever possible try to put things into a more rational context for her. It works best if it's something I was involved in too. That way she can move away from blaming herself for everything."

"She feels guilty about what happened?"

"Guilty about surviving, guilty about not doing enough, always guilty about something. She feels inadequate, worthless. But the reality is, she was so strong."

"That's how people end up taking their own lives."

"They view everything out of context," I said.

"Crazy."

"Not really. Do you know how much she dealt with? I mean, apart from having to talk with Serbs who were responsible for genocide, for prolonging the war?"

"I know about a lot of things…"

We'd stopped on the pavement, and I faced him square-on.

"Sure, you know about the massacre in Ahmici, you told me about her involvement in that," I said. "The marketplace bombings in Sarajevo, the pressure of all that liaison stuff. But when she was investigating war crimes… the things she dealt with there… the sheer inhumanity of it all."

"I can imagine."

"Can you? Can you *really* imagine? The things she's told me, they're beyond imagination. I'm surprised she lasted so long. There are images locked in Bella's mind that are pure evil." I was shaking, and could feel sweat beading on my face. "I've listened to her talk about those things. When she goes into that place, it's like she's staring into the pits of hell. She made her reports, and then kept it all locked away. Nobody ever asked how she was coping, nobody ever allowed her the opportunity to share the experience or rationalise her feelings."

"Until now."

"Until now, with me. Just her and me." I knew that tears were welling in my eyes.

The warrant officer was shifting his weight from foot to foot. He looked uncomfortable, almost guilty. Maybe he was thinking he shouldn't have reached out after all this time, shouldn't be standing there listening to me. I wiped away my tears and began to mumble an apology, but he interrupted.

"I said I had news of Katarina's family."

"And?"

"We kept on looking. Mirsad and Almira - you remember them? They helped too. But there was no word for the longest time."

"You already told me that. What else do you know?"

"I managed to travel into Žepa once everything settled down," said the warrant officer. "Managed to find the farmhouse you visited with the major. It was burned-out. Completely destroyed."

"So the family was killed?" I could feel my heart hardening again. I didn't understand why he would wish to bring me this news. There was nothing in this to help me, and certainly nothing to help Bella.

"I spoke with many people who were evacuated," he said. "Travelled through the refugee camps and eventually discovered the truth." He paused for a moment. "Katarina's mother and her brother didn't survive. I'm sorry. They were pointed out to the Serbs by one of the Muslim families as they tried to board a bus. Separated out and dragged off."

"Their bodies have been found?" My mouth was dry, my words strained.

"The mother's body was recovered. It would seem she was simply shot, which was a blessing of a kind. Adnan's body wasn't found, but witnesses say he was killed at the side of the road trying to defend his mother. The grandparents did get away though. They're in Canada. And there is still hope for the girl, Katarina."

"How's that?"

"Some of the children were smuggled out from Žepa, about a month before the Srebrenica massacre. She was with them. We know that some of the kids got to Goražde, and a few made it into Sarajevo. Not all of them have been traced. She could still be alive."

My heart was racing and my mind span.

"And her father? What of her father?" I managed.

His eyes brightened. "Keep walking."

The day was still drenched with glorious sunlight as we walked across the main road and into Kensington Gardens. The trees were in full bloom.

I was struggling to hold my emotions down. I wanted to shout at this man, push him away. But then I knew what he was trying to do. He wanted me to confront the issue of Katarina and her family, lay it to rest, obtain a sense of proportionality. And I felt he was not so much here to help Isabella, as to help me; because he too had been there, and because he understood.

We reached the Albert Memorial, and there, sat on the steps, was a man with a haggard face who wore the look of someone who had come too far and carried a burden for too long. He stood as we approached, extended his hand and fixed me with his piercing, bright green eyes.

"Hello," he said. "I'm Katarina's father."

I had often wondered what he would be like. Something like his son, I'd always thought; strong, robust and alive. But he seemed fragile and curiously hollow. Perhaps that was inevitable, I thought.

So much pain, so much grief.

The warrant officer left, and I walked slowly across the park with Katarina's father. He asked me to tell him about my journey into Žepa all those years ago. Whom I'd met, what I'd done, what I'd seen.

He had me describe my meeting with his family. What they'd said, what they'd been wearing, how they'd treated me. I realised he was living this story as if it was the last window he would ever have into their lives, so I tried to recall every word and every colour and every scene in intimate detail. Maybe it would help. Maybe it would help us both.

"I read my wife's letter," he said, at length. "The one she gave to you. Your friend Mirsad tracked me down and passed in on to me. I still carry it."

"She was a fine woman."

"She spoke of you, and of the officer who was with you. She said some nice things."

"I can't think why. We couldn't do anything for her, or for your children."

"My wife wrote that Katarina was very excited to see you, and your officer. That she spent the night watching the pair of you sleeping."

"She was a beautiful child."

"She still is."

"You hope to find her?" I asked.

"I know I shall find her."

"You are sure?"

"I have to be sure. There is nothing else."

Children were running through the park. Parents were pushing babies in buggies or prams. Teenagers were lying on the grass, laughing and joking or flirting and kissing. It seemed quite alien to be talking of war and tragedy in this place.

"Your daughter loved you very much," I said. "So did your wife."

"I know. They didn't want me to leave them. But it was my duty. I had to go." He wiped a tear from his eye. He had the look of a man who carries regret and shame. "I should not have left them. I should have stayed. They needed me."

I touched his arm. "It may have made no difference. At least you're still alive. Maybe you should go to Canada, find your wife's parents. They were very proud of you. They told me that."

He nodded. "I will go. But not until I find my daughter."

We were close to the boundary of the park.

"Have you been back to Bosnia?" I asked.

He shook his head. "Not yet. It would be very dangerous. But Mirsad has promised to help. So I will go, eventually. We need to rebuild, help our people to find peace in their hearts. If we can't do that, then there is no hope for my country."

"You really think people can forget all the terrible things that have been done?" I asked.

"I don't think we can ever forget," he said. "Perhaps we shouldn't. It was only a small minority of people who did bad things. Most people just wanted to live their lives, take care of their families. That's what we all have to focus on. That's where hope for the future lies."

"You'll really go back, then?"

"It should be fine."

"You trust Mirsad?"

"Yes."

"He's a good man," I said.

"He is."

He turned to me as we reached the road.

"I came here to thank you for bringing the letter from my wife," he said. "For trying to find me and for caring about my daughter. It was a humanitarian thing to do. I shall carry the letter and these memories with me always."

I thought of all the hatred and barbarity and inhumanity that the war in Bosnia-Herzegovina had spawned, the deceit and cunning and lies that had perpetuated it, that had driven so many of its people beyond the edge of ruin and I could not think what else to say.

This man's life must have been a yawning chasm of despair, but I could see that as long as he kept searching for his daughter, he would not become a shell of a man at all.

There was only one thing left for me to do. I reached around my neck and unclasped the necklace that I'd been wearing ever since that day when I left his family in Žepa.

A cloud passed across the sun. A lump was rising in my throat. It was difficult to say the words.

"Katarina gave this to me… she asked me to give it to you, if we ever met… to tell you that your little princess loves you."

He recognised it instantly. Took it from me and fastened it around his neck with shaking hands. Then he hugged me and sobbed on my shoulder, and told me it is better to move forward with hope in your heart than to be left grieving at the side of a grave.

And, as the rain began to fall and he disappeared into the crowd clutching at his daughter's gift, I knew I could never have told him.

Never have told him that I'd watched a child making her way across the city park, collecting firewood and anything else that may have been of use. That there was something familiar about her slender frame; that I'd adjusted the focus of my binoculars so I could see her more clearly, and that my heart had given a leap for there was no doubt.

I could not tell him that I'd watched the girl reach down and carefully lift a piece of wood as if it were a precious work of art. That she'd placed it in her bag and then glanced straight towards me with her beautiful green eyes; that a fleeting expression of triumph had passed across her pale, perfect face, and that my heart had begun to melt. That she'd smiled her unforgettable smile, and died.

I stood for a long time after Katarina's father had gone, staring blankly into the distance. Then, with fresh summer rain falling onto my face, I left the park and headed home.

x

AUTHOR'S NOTE

More that 1500 children were killed during the Siege of Sarajevo. Hundreds of these were deliberately targeted by snipers.

More than 160 young soldiers from the United Nations Protection Force also lost their lives whilst bringing humanitarian aid to the Balkans, a task of high moral imperative.

Printed in Poland
by Amazon Fulfillment
Poland Sp. z o.o., Wrocław